The Family Man
Gracie Island Book Four
Leigh Fenty

Copyright © 2023 by Leigh Fenty

All rights reserved.

No portion of this book may be reproduced in any form without written permission from the publisher or author, except as permitted by U.S. copyright law.

Chapter One

"The kid has a point."

Jasper was engrossed in paperwork when he glanced up and noticed his son on the other side of the desk, mimicking him. He dropped his pen on the desk, and Jensen did the same. Then Jasper picked up a stack of paper, tapped the ends on the desk, and set them aside. Jensen did the same with his stack of drawings.

When Jensen looked up and met his father's eyes, he smiled and Jasper gave him a wink.

"What do you say we call it a day, Junior Deputy Goodspeed?"

"Yes, sir, Chief."

Jasper laughed. "Come here."

Jensen hopped down from the chair he was kneeling on, ran around the desk and climbed onto Jasper's lap. "Can we go see Mommy now?"

"Yes. Mommy is being a bad girl."

"What did she do?"

"She's working at the bar on her day off."

"Uh oh." He thought for a moment. "Why is that bad?"

"Mommy is supposed to be taking it easy until your baby sister is born."

"Hmm. We better go take her home then."

"I guess we better."

Jensen skipped out of the office and Maisy came from behind the counter and gave him a hug. "Where are you off to, young man?"

"We're going to go get Mommy in trouble."

When Maisy looked at Jasper, he shrugged. "Not literally."

"Okay, you two, I'll see you tonight at the town meeting."

"See ya, Maisy."

Jasper buckled Jensen into his carseat, and got in behind the wheel. They drove the two blocks to The Sailor's Loft and parked on the street. When they approached the flagpole, Jensen stopped at the bell.

"Can I ring it, Daddy?"

"Sure. Three times."

"Why three?" He took hold of the braided rope hanging from the bell and pulled on it three times. "And what's it for, anyway?"

Jasper read the inscription to Jensen.

"Twilight and evening bell

And after that, the dark!

And may there be no sadness of farewell.

When I embark."

"What's that mean?"

Jasper picked up Jensen and sat him on the top rail of the fence around the mast. "It's a sailor's prayer. We ring the bell for people we lost to the sea." When Jensen seemed confused, Jasper added, "People who died in the ocean."

"Oh." Jensen studied the bell for a moment. "Do you know people who died in the ocean?"

"Yes."

"Who?"

Jasper took a moment to debate on whether his five-year-old son was old enough to hear and understand about loss. But he'd already started the conversation. It was too late now to back out. He gave Jensen a smile.

"My great-uncle's fishing boat sunk when I was a kid."

"And he died?"

"Yeah.

"Who else?"

"Someone who isn't family, but I was with him when he died, so I ring the bell for him, too."

"A friend?"

"No. Not really. He wasn't a very good person. But everyone deserves to be remembered."

Jensen thought about it for a moment. "You're nice, Dad."

"Thank you. I try."

"Who else?"

This would be the tough one. Jensen asked once about the picture of his father and the strange woman on Grandma's mantle. At the time, he was young enough to take a simple explanation and not question it further.

"The last one is for my first wife."

Jensen tilted his head the way his mother did. "You had a wife before mommy?"

"Yes. I did. Her name was Ivy."

"And she...drownded in the sea?"

"Yes."

Jensen jumped to the ground and hugged Jasper around the waist. "Do you think Grandma has cookies?"

Jasper smiled. "Grandma always has cookies."

"Can we get some?"

Jasper checked his watch. "As long as we don't tell Mommy we ate them so close to dinner."

They entered the restaurant and Aunt Peg greeted them both with a hug. She looked at Jensen. "My goodness, did you grow since I saw you last?"

Jensen giggled. "You saw me this morning."

"I swear you've grown. Even since this morning."

Jasper glanced toward the bar. "How long has she been here?"

"About an hour. I tried to convince her to go home."

"Can you take this little man to the kitchen? He's hoping grandma has a cookie for him."

Peg took Jensen's hand. "I believe she just pulled some out of the oven."

Jasper watched them go, before going into the bar. Poppie was stacking clean glasses near the beer taps. He cleared his throat, and she turned to him.

"I know what you're going to say."

"We had a deal."

She nodded and rubbed her lower back. "Monday and Wednesday afternoon, and Friday evening with you."

"And today is…"

"Tuesday."

He sat on a stool.

"Can I offer you a beer to distract you?" He shook his head as she looked behind him. "Where's my son?"

"*Our* son is getting a cookie from Grandma."

Poppie checked her watch. "This close to dinner?"

"About the deal."

"I'm sorry. But Mark came in early because there was no one to work."

"Did Peg call you?"

"No. I called to see who was working, and I got Mark."

"It's not that I don't want you to work. I know you love the bar. But we decided after six months you'd quit. Here it is two months later and you're still working three days a week."

She put her hands on the bar and leaned toward him. "I'm going to miss it." She straightened and rubbed her belly. "After this third one. I won't be working anymore."

"Speaking of the third one, where's the second one?"

"Sarah has him. And yes, she reprimanded me, too."

"If you really want to work, we can figure it out. After a few months, anyway."

Mark came in from the storeroom carrying a case of beer. He set it down and walked to them. "I tried to tell her to go home."

"Not your fault, Mark. My wife's a stubborn woman." He looked at her. "Can we go home now, please? Town meeting is in two hours."

"Yes." She took off the black apron she could barely tie behind her back. "What's Mayor Steel's big announcement?"

"I've no idea." When she raised an eyebrow, he added, "Really. I don't know." They collected Jensen, then Jasper and Jensen followed Poppie to Sarah and Lewis' house."

After they got married, Jasper got rid of the car Poppie brought from Boston and got her a Jeep Cherokee with the insurance money received for his totaled Jeep. James insisted Jasper keep the Bronco, so it became his official sheriff's department vehicle. James bought himself a small four-wheel-drive truck, which he rarely drove. Since he and Kat lived right in town, they could walk most anywhere they wanted to go.

When they pulled up to the house, Sarah was on the porch with baby Alice in her arms, and Tucker, Matty, and Micha on the porch. Like Jasper and Poppie, she and Lewis had two boys, followed by a girl. All of them were born a few months ahead of the corresponding Goodspeed children.

Sarah gave them a wave and followed the boys as they ran to say hi. At two and a half, Tucker had trouble navigating the steps, and she took his hand and helped him. Jasper got out of the Bronco and picked up Tucker.

He smiled at Sarah. "Thank you. Hopefully this will be the last unplanned babysitting gig."

"Poppie helps me a lot more than I help her." She watched the kids giggling with Jensen in the Bronco. "Besides, these guys couldn't handle it if they spent a day without their cousins."

"Did you ever envision this seven years ago when you, Lewis, and I were single and playing music together on Friday nights?"

"Me and Lewis, yes. You? No way." She patted Tucker's back, then went to Poppie's window, while Jasper put Tucker in the backseat of the Cherokee. When he got into the Bronco, Sarah rounded her brood onto the porch, and they all waved as Jasper and Poppie drove away.

Jasper was following Poppie and was teaching Jensen the words to one of the old sea shanties he sang with Uncle Lewis and Aunt Sarah. But when Poppie's Cherokee suddenly swerved to the side of the road, he pulled in behind her.

"Stay in the car, bud."

Jensen had learned to do what his father said. "Okay, Dad."

Jasper got out of the Bronco and opened Poppie's door. "What's wrong?"

"I think I got a flat."

"Stay there, I'll check it."

Poppie still hadn't learned to always do what Jasper told her to do. She lumbered out of the Jeep and followed him to the right front tire.

He glanced at her. "Penelope?"

"Sorry. I wanted to see."

Tucker seemed to believe he'd been abandoned and he started crying.

Jasper shook his head. "I generally have a reason for telling you to do something."

She smiled. "I thought you just got off on it."

"Go check on our son."

She opened the door. "Tucker, my sweet baby boy. What're you crying for? Mommy's right here."

Jasper came up behind her. "I'm here too. Although, I know I don't rate as high as Mommy does."

Tucker's crying turned into intermittent sobs as Jasper moved Poppie out of the way and reached in to release his seatbelt holding the carseat in place. "Do you want to ride in Daddy's truck? Lots of fun."

Tucker smiled and Jasper removed him and the seat from the Cherokee and carried them to the Bronco. He strapped the seat next to Jensen, then turned to Poppie.

"I'll come change the tire in the morning. Or more likely, I'll have Willis do it. Do you have everything?"

Poppie held up her purse and the diaper bag. "This is it."

He took the bag from her, then opened the door. She had a bit of trouble getting in, so Jasper gave her some help.

"Up you go."

She put a hand on his chest. "Remember the time you rescued me from Lewis' truck? Picked me up like it was nothing?"

"Yes. I do."

"I'm never going to be that tiny little thing you loved to tease."

"I love you tiny, pregnant, getting over being pregnant, and thinking about getting pregnant again."

"That's been our life for six years."

"Yes it has. And I'm fine with that."

"But the day we got married, you said you wanted to wait a year or five to have a baby."

"We'd been married for an hour. I was still letting it soak in."

"But instead of waiting five years, we had three kids in five years."

Jasper gave Jensen a wink. "You're right. Maybe we could get rid of those two in the backseat and start fresh with little Miss Goodspeed."

Jensen giggled. "You can't get rid of us."

"Why not?"

"Because we're too cute."

Jasper laughed. "The kid has a point."

Poppie nodded. "They are pretty cute."

"The new ones might not turn out so cute. We'd be stuck with not-so-cute kids."

Poppie glanced over her shoulder. "We wouldn't want that. We might as well keep these two."

"Okay, cute boys." He kissed Poppie. "And beautiful Mommy. Let's go home to our not-so- cute dogs."

"Don't say that about our two furry sons and daughter. They're the cutest dogs ever."

"Okay, okay. You're right. We'll keep them around a while longer, too."

While Poppie warmed some left-over chili and corn bread she got from Kat, Jasper took the boys and the dogs to the beach. Jasper carried Tucker from the house, but once they got to the sand, the baby wanted down.

"Okay, but let's try to stay relatively clean and dry so we don't need to change you before the town meeting."

Tucker looked up at him, gave him a drooly smile, before falling on his bottom in the wet sand.

Jasper sighed. "Okay. One down." He helped Tucker stand, and took his hand, as they walked slowly down the beach while Jensen and the dogs ran ahead. He called to Jensen. "Slow down. I don't want you to fall and get dirty."

When Jensen stopped and turned around to give Jasper a wave, Sam came racing up and jumped on him. Jensen hit the sand and the big dog playfully attacked him. Blackjack limped over and joined in, while Penny ran around the three of them and barked.

Jasper shook his head. "Two for two."

Chapter Two

"Are you teaching my son to play poker?"

Jasper got the boys changed into dry pants while Poppie served dinner. All three of her men loved her chili and grandma's cornbread, so everyone would be happy. She liked the chili too, but it seemed baby girl Goodspeed didn't. So she thawed a frozen burrito for herself. She'd been craving them for the last three months.

When Jasper brought the boys in and put Tucker in his highchair, he smiled at her. "Burritos again?"

Poppie shrugged. "Baby wants what baby wants."

"We really need to give her a name."

"We will. We've got two more months to think about it."

"The boys were named months before they arrived."

"I know. But this is our little girl, and it needs to be perfect." She smiled at her sons. "Your names are perfect as well. They were just easier to come up with."

Jensen was too busy eating his chili to care much one way or the other. While Tucker was attempting to pick up a bean from the tray of his highchair.

Jasper put it in Tucker's mouth. "I don't know what Thomas is announcing, but I need to give an update on the storm."

"How's it looking?"

"So far, it's hanging out in the middle of the Atlantic. They're not even calling it a hurricane yet. And it's moving more south than west at this point."

"And hurricane Emilio was headed north. But that didn't work out so well."

"True. You never can tell what they're going to do."

"It better stay out there and away from us. One hurricane is enough for me."

Jensen suddenly tuned into the conversation. "What's a hurricane?"

Jasper gave him a smile. "It's a big storm in the ocean. Sometimes, they come onto land and bring lots of wind and rain."

Jensen shrugged. "Like winter?"

"Yeah. Just like winter. Only a little worse." Jasper finished his chili and ate his last bite of cornbread. "Okay. Let's finish up. Don't want to be late."

Poppie stood and felt a sharp pain in her back. She leaned on the table, and Jasper got to his feet and went to her.

She glanced at him. "I'm okay. My back has been bothering me today."

Jasper rubbed her lower back. "Why don't you stay home with Tucker and I'll take Jensen with me to the meeting?"

Poppie straightened. "I'm fine. I want to go." She arched her back a little, then picked up her dishes. When she tried to pick up more, Jasper stopped her.

"I got this. Please, go sit for a few minutes."

"Just let me clean up Tucker."

"Penelope. I got it. Go sit down."

She frowned at him. "Penelope, huh?"

He smiled. "Go."

She sat on the couch, while she listened to Jasper get the boys and the kitchen cleaned up. He was a great father. She knew he would be. But he'd passed all expectations. He was much more patient than she was. And when the boys needed to be disciplined, which wasn't often, he was calm and fair about dealing out consequences. He was also a big kid at heart, so she'd often find him and Jensen getting into mischief, or playing together like they were best friends.

When he came to see her, he seemed to sense she'd been thinking about him.

"What?"

"I love you."

"I love you, too." He sat down. "Are you sure you're okay to go tonight?"

"Yes." She took his hand. "I told Sarah I'd help her with the snacks."

"Honey."

"I'll sit on a stool."

Tucker climbed onto Jasper's lap. "Shoe."

"Are you ready to go?"

Tucker nodded, and Jasper set him on the floor. "Go get your shoes."

He wandered off in search of his shoes, and Jensen brought his tennis shoes and sat next to Jasper. He hadn't quite mastered tying them yet. So he slipped them on, then put his feet in Jasper's lap.

Jasper tied them. "Go help your brother find his shoes or we'll never get out of here. And go pee."

"I don't need to pee."

Jasper studied him for a moment. "Just try."

Jensen sighed. "Okay."

Jasper looked at Poppie. "Every time."

"He likes the bathrooms at the Ice House."

"Your son is weird."

"So now he's my son?"

"When he's being weird, yeah." He held his hand out to her. "You go pee too."

Poppie let him pull her to her feet. "Don't worry. I don't like the bathrooms at the Ice House."

"But you'll be using them tonight." He looked at his watch. "In about an hour and a half."

She shook her head. "Do you wanna bet?"

"Five bucks."

"You're on."

Tucker brought his shoes to Jasper, then held his arms out. "I don't suppose you'd like to go pee like a big boy before we go?"

Tucker shook his head and Jasper and looked at Poppie. "Eventually he'll do it, right?"

"Eventually."

Jasper and the family arrived at the Ice House a few minutes before the meeting started. There was a big crowd tonight. Probably half the town was there, eager to hear the mayor's announcement and get an update on the storm.

Jasper had asked Quinn to check for the latest storm information before coming to the meeting. Quinn made his way to them when they entered the room.

"Were you able to get online?"

"Yeah. I printed it for you."

Jasper read the paper. The weather disturbance was still in the tropical storm category, but the wind speed was picking up. If it kept increasing at the same rate, it'd officially be a hurricane by tomorrow. It'd also slowed down and was now heading in a southwestern direction.

"Okay, thanks."

Quinn studied him for a moment. "What do you think? Are we going to get hit?"

"Too soon to tell. Let's take a seat." Poppie found three seats a few rows from the front of the room. Jasper joined them and put Tucker on his lap as Mayor Steele went to the podium.

Thomas raised his hands. "Okay, folks, let's get settled and get the meeting over with so you can get to the snacks. I know that's why you all came tonight."

The crowd laughed in agreement as the last stragglers took their seats.

Thomas adjusted the microphone. "We've got a little town business to discuss, then Chief Goodspeed will give us an update on the storm."

Someone yelled. "We're here for your announcement, Tom."

Thomas laughed. "First things first. We got most of Main Street painted over the summer and we've got a few more weeks..." He held up his hand and crossed his fingers, "...of good weather before the winter rains start. So we expect to make it to the movie theater. Speaking of which, the community theater group has expressed concern over the soundness of the stage. So we need a couple volunteers to shore it up or build a new one. Maisy will have the details. You can call her at the station."

Thomas spent another ten minutes before he got to his announcement. "Okay. I'm afraid your expectations might exceed what I'm about to say." He cleared his throat. "East Maine Connects was here last week about putting up a relay tower, which might provide cell phone service here on the island."

The announcement was met with more dissension than excitement.

Thomas held up his hands. "I expected your response. But I felt it should be put to a vote. Instead of holding a verbal vote here tonight, we're going to put boxes around town, in the usual spots, to allow everyone a chance to be heard. At best, all they can offer is the possibility. With our weather, it'll be a rough undertaking. So I wanted feedback before the town puts out money for something that may not work."

The noise level rose as everyone discussed the matter with those sitting near them.

"Okay. I know you want to talk about this, but let's wait until after the meeting. The boxes will go out tomorrow and stay up for a week. We'll post the results on the City Hall bulletin board." He waved at Jasper. "Chief, are you ready to come up?"

Jasper stood and set Tucker in the chair, before going to the podium. Thomas put a hand on the mic and leaned in toward Jasper's ear. "I expected dissension, but I think they're about ready to string me up from the mast in front of the Loft.

Jasper patted his shoulder. "Maisy would never let that happen." The mayor stepped down and Jasper smiled at the crowd. "I know what you're all thinking. And I'm thinking it, too. We've managed this long without cell service. No need for it now."

He got a round of cheers from the crowd.

"But Mayor Steel is just doing his job, which is letting you all decide." He took the paper from his pocket. "I have an update on the tropical storm. It's still pretty far off the coast, but it's getting stronger. The sustained winds are pushing sixty, which brings it closer to hurricane status. And she has a name. Isabella. Let's hope Isabella doesn't come to visit."

When he spotted Tucker headed down the aisle toward him, he laughed. "Looks like my helper is here." He stepped off the platform and picked up Tucker, then returned to the podium. "We'll post updates at City Hall and at the Loft. It if turns toward us, we'll fly the yellow flag and there'll be an emergency town meeting. But we'll give you lots of warning. Hopefully Isabella will behave better than Emilio did." He put a hand on Tucker's arm as the baby tried to touch the mic. "I guess that's about it. I think this boy is ready for a cookie."

Tucker looked at him. "Cookie."

"What did I tell you?"

Jasper stepped down and was met by a group of people worried about the storm. As he fielded questions, Poppie came and took Tucker from him. He did his best to appease their fears, but after getting hit by the tail end of Emilio seven years ago, they had a right to be concerned.

After fifteen minutes, he broke free, and found Sarah by herself, getting help from Jensen and Micha, who were six weeks apart in age.

Jasper came up to the table. "Where's Poppie? She said she was helping you."

"She is. She had to pee."

Jasper grinned. "Of course she did. Do you want me to take those two helpers?"

"No. They're fine. You might track down Lewis though. He's got Matty, Alice, and Tucker. You'd probably be a welcome sight."

"Sure thing." When he spotted Poppie coming out of the restroom, he folded his arms across his chest.

She smiled. "Shut up."

"You owe me five bucks."

"I'll pay you later."

"Are we talking trade? Or...?"

"I'll pay you in whatever form you'd like."

He winked at her, as he took her hand and pulled her in close. "I'll come up with something."

He gave her a kiss, patted her stomach, then left to find Lewis and the kids. He found them sitting on the floor. Lewis was holding Alice and dealing cards to the kids with one hand.

"Are you teaching my son to play poker?"

"If he had any money, I'd think about it."

Tucker saw Jasper, and he got to his feet and ran to him. Jasper took the card out of his mouth and tossed it to Lewis. The crowd was dispersing and the two men took the kids to Poppie and Sarah.

Tucker held his arms out to Poppie and she took him with a groan. "You're getting so heavy." She kissed him, then set him down. Most everyone was gone, so the kids took off running around the big empty space, while Lewis and Jasper helped the women clean up and pack the leftover snacks.

Jasper glanced at a wooden stool. "So, how much time did you actually spend sitting on the stool?"

"About five minutes. Turns out, sitting on that thing was much harder on my back than standing."

Sarah rubbed Poppie's back. "Have you talked to Dr. Hannigan about your back pain?"

"Not yet. But it's been slowly getting worse, so I'll ask him about it next week when I go in for my by-monthly checkup."

"I'm glad he's keeping an eye on you."

"Well, it seems these kids like to pop right out of me when they're ready, so he doesn't want any surprises."

Sarah watched the kids for a moment. "Don't rub it in. I was in labor for fourteen hours with Alice."

Lewis put an arm around her waist. "Yeah, that was rough."

She stepped away and frowned at him. "I don't remember you being in labor."

He kissed her on the cheek. "You're right. But I walked, and paced, and stood, and nearly got my hand broken for fourteen hours."

She patted his chest. "You're right, honey. It's totally the same thing."

Jasper packed the last of the cookies into a plastic tote. "Okay. Let's round up these kids so I can get my very pregnant wife home and in bed." He whistled, and the kids all stopped and looked at him. "Time to go."

They all ran back, but Tucker didn't quite make it, and he fell ten feet before he got to them. Poppie started for him, but Jasper stopped her. "You need to stop carrying him. He's getting too heavy."

"Tell him that."

Jasper picked up Tucker. To console the crying, he gave the baby the flashlight off his belt. "Here you go, bud." The crying stopped and the two families left the building and headed home.

Chapter Three

"Is that a scientific conclusion or wishful thinking?"

On Monday and Wednesday afternoons, and Friday nights, Jasper helped Poppie at the bar. Since the kids came along, she only worked afternoon shifts. She'd slowly cut back from five days a week, to three, and now to two. She was supposed to stop altogether by her sixth month. Poppie being Poppie, that didn't happen. So Jasper left the office at noon on those two days to work the bar with her. The other days were covered by a few people on a rotating basis. Beryl would come in and work if no one else was available. Mark covered the nights, except for Friday, his one night off. Jasper planned to continue working Friday nights, even after he convinced Poppie to stop. Fridays were busy and needed to be covered by someone who knew what they were doing. He enjoyed it, liked visiting with the patrons, and still got to play some music.

After catching her working yesterday, Jasper tried his best to convince Poppie to stay home for their Wednesday shift, but she insisted on working one more afternoon at the bar with him. When they were in the Jeep and on their way into town, he glanced at her.

"How did I end up with such a stubborn woman?"

She smiled. "Just lucky, I guess. And I believe we're pretty evenly matched in the stubbornness department."

"Hmm. I don't agree."

"Which proves my point." She reached over and squeezed his thigh, then continued her way up until he grabbed her hand.

"Penelope, I swear. You've been a very bad girl lately."

"Just lately?"

"More so than usual. Seems you get like this around month seven of your pregnancies."

She pulled her hand away. "Are you complaining?"

"No. I want to get into town without wrapping the Jeep around a tree because my wife can't keep her hands to herself."

She folded her hands in her lap. "I'll behave. But tonight, watch out."

"We really should be a little careful at this point."

She nodded. "I'm fine with being careful." She smiled. "I'll carefully attack you tonight when the boys are in bed."

Jasper sighed as he pulled into the Loft parking lot. "I'm okay with that. As long as you're careful."

He helped her out of the Jeep, and Peg greeted them at the door.

"Jasper, I thought you'd be working alone today."

He glanced at Poppie. "So did I. Do you want to try to tell her to go home?"

"No. I'll let you two work that out."

"Has it been busy?"

"No. I don't expect you'll have too much to do. I only made three drinks during lunch."

"Okay, good. I can at least stock the bar for Mark."

"There's also an order back there that needs to be put away."

"Oh, yay. My favorite thing to do."

Poppie put a hand on his arm. "But you're so good at it."

He took her hand. "Come on, honey. Let's get to work."

They went behind the bar and Poppie sat on a stool to cut limes and lemons, while Jasper continued to the storeroom and frowned at the order.

He picked up a box cutter and opened a box of rum, then put the bottles in the correct spot on the shelf. While he was on the third box, he heard someone at the bar. He left to see who it was and try to intercept Poppie. But he was too late. She was up and pouring two drafts for the Murphy brothers.

Doyle and Reece were twins, and bigger than Jasper in weight and height. They'd gone to school with him and barely earned their diplomas, but they ran their own fishing boat together. Ninety percent of the time, they were docile. The other ten percent, they weren't. But they only fought with each other. If you happened to get in the middle of it, though, you could get hurt. Both Jasper and Lewis had gotten too close in the past. Today, they seemed in good spirits, and this was probably their first beer of the day.

Reece smiled at Jasper. "Afternoon, Chief."

"Are you guys done for the day already?"

"Seems that tropical storm has the fish spooked. We couldn't catch a damn thing."

"It's pretty far away still."

Doyle nodded. "Sure, but the fish know. It's coming our way."

Jasper hoped Doyle's prediction was just an excuse for a bad day of fishing. But the men who spent every day on the water, seemed to sense something was coming long before the weathermen reported it.

"I hope you're wrong."

Doyle repeated. "The fish know."

Jasper took the beers from Poppie and set them in front of the Murphy brothers.

"Next customer, call me."

"Are you banishing me to my stool and cutting board?"

"Not banishing. Asking you politely to take it easy."

"I've cut more citrus than Mark will need."

"You can come watch me put the order away."

She smiled. "Oh. Yes. I like that."

Jasper shook his head. "Would you like me to take my shirt off while I do it?"

"Now you're just teasing me." She rubbed her stomach.

"Are you okay?"

"Yes." She sat on two stacked cases of beer. "Just a Braxton Hicks."

"I want to know who the hell Braxton Hicks is and why they named false contractions after him."

"I wonder if his mother was proud of him. 'That's my boy. The father of fake labor pains.'"

Jasper smiled. "I'm sure she was."

"Do you think Jensen and Tucker will be famous for something?"

"Probably not."

"That's okay. We'll be proud of them no matter what they do."

"That's right."

"Do you think they'll want to be Gracie Island deputies one day?"

"Only if they want to."

"Of course." She considered it for a moment. "Did you want to?"

"Become a deputy?"

"Yeah."

"When I was a kid, I thought it was pretty great. But when I got old enough to figure out my dad was, well, the way my dad was, I changed my mind. Then, I'm a senior in high school and I realize how limited my options were if I wanted to stay on the island. I was kind of a shoe in for deputy, being a Goodspeed and all."

"So you left for Augusta and went to sheriff school."

"Yes. And the rest is history."

"I hope our boys and this little girl stay here."

"They will."

"How do you know?"

"Because they're descended from the Gracies. It's in their blood."

"I hope you're right."

"Penelope, I'm always right."

"Except that's whiskey and you're putting it in with the scotch."

He looked at the bottle. "You distracted me."

By three o'clock, they'd only had a few more customers. Most of them fishermen who'd called it a day when the fish weren't cooperating. Like the Murphy brothers, they blamed it on the weather.

At four, Lewis came in. He sat at the bar and Poppie set a bottle of beer in front of him.

"You look tired."

"Alice was fussy last night. Sarah says she's teething, but she's only three months old. Whatever it is, she was up most of the night."

"And by that, you mean Sarah was up with her all night?"

"Yeah. But I can't sleep if Sarah's not in bed with me."

"You're the worst."

"I am not. I got up with the boys this morning and fed them breakfast. Alice finally conked out around five and I let Sarah sleep in. I didn't leave for work until almost ten."

"Okay. I guess that's helpful."

"I'm a good father, sis."

She smiled. "I know you are. I'm actually very impressed."

He looked at Jasper. "Is she being a smart ass, or is she serious?"

Jasper shrugged. "I never know for sure."

"So what's with the weather? The talk at the marina is it's coming this way."

"As of this morning, it's still out there a ways and headed south. It could very well peter out in the Atlantic and never hit land."

"Is that a scientific conclusion or wishful thinking?"

"A little of both, I guess."

Poppie went around the bar and sat next to Lewis. "Don't put hurricane vibes out there. No hurricane. Isabella will be a good little tropical storm and go somewhere else."

Lewis pointed at her. "Now that's wishful thinking."

Poppie sat up straight on the stool. "Oh my gosh. I feel so guilty."

"Why?"

"The three of us are here at the bar and Sarah's at home with our five children."

"Do you want me to take you home?"

She glanced at Jasper. "I don't feel that guilty. Besides, Jasper might need help."

Jasper looked around the empty bar. "Pretty sure I can handle it."

"You might get a rush."

"On a Wednesday afternoon?"

"You never know."

"Let Lewis take you home. Mark will be here at six."

She sighed. "Fine.

On the way home, Poppie turned and looked at Lewis.

"I really am proud of you. You're a good father."

He glanced at her. "Wow. Thank you. Did you doubt I would be?"

"No. I always knew once you settle down you'd do it right, when you found the right woman."

"Where's this coming from? Is this because you're pregnant and all hormonal?"

"No. I mean it."

"In that case, thank you. Honestly, I had my doubts when Sarah told me she was pregnant with Micha. But I really love it. And I love that you're here and we're raising our kids together. I never saw that coming. It took me six years to get you to visit me here."

"Then you couldn't get me to leave."

"I never wanted you to leave. I knew the moment you met Jasper, that was it."

"I got lucky."

"You did. And don't you forget it."

"Never."

"But, so did he."

"Aww. You do love me."

"I've never said otherwise."

Chapter Four

"It's more of a statistical problem."

Poppie sighed, then snuggled closer to Jasper. These days, the only way she could get close to him in bed was to put her back to him.

He kissed the back of her neck. "What's up?"

"I feel like a cow. And I still have two months to go."

"You're not a cow. Maybe a calf. A very small calf."

"Thank you."

She rolled onto her back. "Why am I so much bigger this time? And why is she giving me so much grief?"

Jasper put a hand on her belly. "Every pregnancy is different. You told me that when you were pregnant with Tucker."

"Do you think it's because she's a girl?"

"Probably not." He moved his hand around her stomach, trying to feel the baby's movement.

Poppie took his hand and moved it to her side. "Right there. She loves to kick me in the ribs."

Jasper smiled. "This is so weird. I'm kind of jealous my part in all this took, what? A minute?"

"I'll trade. You can carry the baby and I'll do what you do."

"Um...No. I'm good. I could never do it. I'll stick to my one-minute contribution."

She was quiet for a few minutes while they felt the baby kick. "I'm beginning to rethink the four kids plan."

Jasper laughed. "You also said that when you were pregnant with Tucker."

"Did I? I don't remember. I'll see how I feel after this baby girl comes. If she ever comes."

"This baby needs a name."

"Not Petunia."

When they found out the baby was a girl, Jasper suggested the name Petunia as a joke. But Poppie was so against it, he brought it up often to tease her. "It's a great name."

"No, it's not. Petunia is the name of a pig. If you want to name something Petunia, we'll get a pig."

"No, I could never do that. I'd have to give up eating bacon."

Poppie looked at her stomach. "I miss my toes. Are they still there?"

"Yes, my love. They're still there."

"You know what else I miss?"

"Hmm?"

"S-E-X."

"The kids are asleep. You don't need to spell it."

"Remember when we used to have insane sex?"

"Not insane sex. An insane amount of sex."

"Either way."

"We'll have insane sex again."

"Promise?"

"I promise. You should get some sleep."

"I want to come up with a name first."

Jasper rose onto his elbow and rested his head on his hand. After a moment, he sat up. "I got it." She frowned, and he said, "No, really. It's perfect. I can't believe we didn't think of it sooner."

"Okay. What is it?"

"Gracie."

She took his arm. "Oh, my gosh. It *is* perfect."

"I know."

"Gracie Goodspeed. It's the most perfect name ever."

"She needs a middle name. You know, so when we reprimand her like Jasper Tucker Goodspeed, did you just track mud into my kitchen?"

Poppie smiled. "Did you track mud into your mother's kitchen?"

"Many, many times. That's why I built a mud room for our house."

"Because you knew we were going to have children someday who'd track mud into the kitchen?"

"I guess subconsciously, yes. I didn't even know I was building the house for you until I saw you in it. And then I realized every decision had been with you in mind."

"Yet, you barely talked to me for the ten months I was gone."

"I've apologized for that."

She kissed him. "I know. So a middle name. How about May? It's my mother's middle name and my grandmother's first name."

"I love it. Gracie May Goodspeed." He laid back down and Poppie rolled onto her side. "And I love you."

"I love you, too. And Gracie May is going to be a good girl. She'll never track mud into my kitchen,"

"I'm sure you're right. Can we go to sleep now?"

"If you're done talking."

"Me?"

"Goodnight, Jasper."

Poppie hadn't slept well for a few months now, but the last few weeks had been worse. She couldn't get comfortable, and no matter how she laid, after a while, her back would start aching. Everything about this pregnancy felt different. With both of the boys, it was a breeze. No morning sickness, no cravings, and she gained barely more than the expected twenty-five pounds. With Gracie, she'd already gained thirty. And on her small frame, that was a lot. She'd been craving frozen burritos for far too long. And she'd suffered from morning sickness her first three months.

She rubbed her stomach. "It's okay, Gracie May. I forgive you. I know as soon as I see your sweet face, all will be forgotten. Gracie May. I love that name so much."

She glanced at Jasper, who was sleeping soundly. He looked pretty cute. Really, really cute.

She rubbed his leg.

He mumbled, "What?"

"I miss you."

He kissed her neck. "I'm right here."

She rolled onto her back. "I haven't been told specifically not to…"

Jasper opened his eyes, then raised onto an elbow. "It's not so much a matter of should we, or shouldn't we. It's more of a statistical problem."

Poppie put a hand on his face. "Well, you've always been good at solving problems."

"That's true. Let me see what I can figure out."

Tucker woke at his usual eight o'clock and Poppie went to get him changed and give him a bottle. Like the potty training, weaning from the bottle was an ongoing struggle. But they'd gotten him down to one in the morning when he woke up. Jasper could sometimes get him to take a cup, but Poppie usually handled the mornings, and she hadn't tried as hard as she should have to wean him to the cup. She enjoyed their early morning cuddle. But soon she'd have a newborn, and Tucker would need to share his mommy.

She sat in the rocking chair by the fireplace and cuddled her youngest son. He was a big boy and there was barely room on her lap for him. But just as Jasper had solved the problem last night, Tucker always figured out how to get comfortable on his mommy's lap.

While Poppie tended to Tucker, Jasper took a shower and got dressed for work. They'd fallen into a routine, and accept for an occasional hiccup, life in the Goodspeed house was peaceful and uneventful. Jasper was happier than he ever imagined he could be and he was glad life on Gracie Island was generally uneventful, too. It allowed him to spend time with his family. Time he wouldn't have living anywhere else.

When he came into the kitchen, Poppie handed him a cup of coffee. Being a non-coffee drinker, it'd taken her a while to learn how to make it the way he liked it. But now, she was a pro, and his first cup was always at home instead of at the station. He took the oversized mug with him as he picked up Penny and let the two big dogs out the French Doors.

Sam jumped off the deck and ran toward the beach, while Blackjack took the steps. He still had a limp from the truck accident. It didn't slow him down too much, but he wasn't able to keep up with Sam. Penny was still spoiled and living up to her formal name, Princess Penny.

When he reached the sand, Jasper set Penny down to do her business, then sat on the bench he'd put there several years ago. He studied the horizon. The sky was oddly clear, something that rarely happened on the island. And the wave pattern was different. The swell seemed a little higher, and the waves were coming ashore faster than normal. The weather was definitely brewing into something. It was just too soon to determine how bad it'd be. His shoulder was a little achy, too, which meant it was going to rain.

When he heard Poppie and the boys coming up behind him, Jasper stood and took Tucker from her arms.

"You really need to quit carrying him. Especially down here on the sand."

She watched Jasper set him on the bench. "He's still my baby boy."

"Your very heavy, baby boy." He motion toward the bench. "Take a load off."

She sat next to Tucker and looked at Jasper. "You're a worrywart."

"Always have been. You've known that since you met me."

She smiled. "Yes. I have. And ninety percent of the time, I find it charming."

"And what about the other ten?"

"Annoying."

He smiled at her. "Charmingly annoying?"

"Maybe."

Jasper looked at the boys. "We should get these guys back before they get dirty."

"Good call." She held out a hand, and Jasper pulled her to her feet, then he whistled for the dogs.

Penny hadn't gone far, and she came to his feet and whined. Blackjack showed up next, and nosed Jasper's knee, leaving a wet sandy print on his uniform.

"Thanks, Blackjack."

Poppie laughed. "It wouldn't be a normal day if you didn't go to work with either sand, mud, or something from Tucker's mouth on your uniform."

They headed for the house with Jasper carrying Tucker, and Jensen holding Penny. Sam would come along as soon as he realized they were leaving him behind.

For the last month or so, Jasper wanted to save Poppie from making him breakfast, so he'd been getting it at The Sailor's Loft on his way to the station. Peg greeted him when he came through the door.

"Good morning, honey. What sounds good today?"

Jasper took a moment. "Pancakes. A couple of scrambled eggs. Bacon or sausage. Either, or both." He smiled. "I'm hungry this morning." He checked his watch. "I'm also running late, so can I get it to go?"

"Of course."

"Is Mom around?"

"She and James took the early ferry to pick up some supplies. She'll be back before lunch."

He sat at a table and Peg brought him some coffee to drink while he waited. When he spotted Thomas coming through the door, Jasper waved him over to the table.

"Good morning, Chief."

"Morning, Mayor."

Thomas Steele was Jasper's second cousin, but he'd always referred to him by his first name. When Thomas became mayor six years ago, out of respect for the position, Jasper started calling him Mayor Steele. It was an expected formality on the island, and it was why everyone but Jasper's immediate family called him Chief, even though most of the town had known him all his life.

Thomas sat across from Jasper. "How do you think the cell phone vote will go once everyone's had time to mull it over?"

"Some people will warm up to the idea. But probably not enough to warrant the expense. It seems to me the service will be sporadic at best. Probably more of a nuisance than anything else."

"That's about what I figured, too. We'll revisit it every year or so. Someday it might happen." He nodded at Peg when she brought him a coffee. "Wouldn't it make your job a little easier? Make you more available?"

"Not sure I want to be more available. Everyone knows where to find me. I'm usually in radio range, at the station, here, or home. It might be nice to extend the range. So if that ever comes up for a vote, I'd be onboard."

"A taller tower?"

"Yes. Really tall. It'd be great to have radio beyond Harper's Fork."

"I'll keep it in mind."

Peg returned with Jasper's meal and he stood. "I'll call you in a while with a storm update."

"Thanks, Chief. What's your gut feeling on this? I know you're weirdly connected to the weather around here."

"I haven't gotten a read on it yet, but I went to the beach this morning, and something's up. We're sure to get some sort of weather out of this."

"How's the shoulder?"

"My shoulder says it's going to rain."

"Okay. Keep me posted."

Chapter Five

"Is your weather spidy sense kicking in?"

When Jasper got to the office a few minutes after nine, Quinn was talking to Maisy.

Jasper stopped inside the door. "One of these days, I'm going to beat both of you here."

Maisy smiled at him. "Sweetheart, I'm not sure we could handle that."

Quinn picked up his coffee mug. "I'll go get the computer going. With the clear weather, maybe we'll have good service today."

"I hope so. I'm concerned about the tropical storm. I'd like to see what she's up to."

Quinn nodded as he headed for his office and Maisy patted Jasper's hand. "Go eat your breakfast while it's hot. The storm news can wait twenty minutes."

"Thanks, Maisy." He headed for his office. "I saw your husband at the Loft. Did you send him off without breakfast this morning?"

Maisy put her hands on her hips. "I've opened this office every morning at eight o'clock for nearly thirty years. Thomas knows he only gets a hot breakfast on the weekends."

Jasper bowed down to her. "You are the glue holding this office together."

"And don't you forget it, young man. I still remember Kat bringing you in here when you were barely older than Jensen."

"I'm well aware. And I love you for it. That and your coffee. And your cookies." He thought for a moment. "And the fact you still call me sweetheart, even though I'm thirty-six years old."

"And I'll never stop."

"I'm going to hold you to that." He headed for his office and sat behind his desk. Someday, Maisy would retire. He had no idea what he'd do then. She was irreplaceable.

When he finished his breakfast and poured himself a third cup of coffee, he checked with Quinn for any updated information on the storm. He stood next to Quinn's chair as they both read the newly posted update on the storm.

It was now classified as a hurricane, with the winds nearing eighty miles per hour. The direction had stayed the same and with its current path it'd make landfall well south of them. But it'd slowed down. If it continued to move southwest, they'd be okay. If it moved in a more westerly direction, they could get hit by the outer rim.

"I want you to check every hour. If it heads west, let me know."

"Yes, sir."

Jasper glanced at Quinn, who seemed to have a question. "What?"

"What happens if it heads west?"

"Then we'll be in some trouble. How much trouble will depend on if and when it turns."

"Okay. I'll keep an eye on it."

Jasper put a hand on his shoulder. "Keeping on top of it will be the key to being ready for whatever Isabella has in store for us. As piss pour as our internet is, we've got a lot more information than they did for the last big one. And the one that hit in 1905 was a complete surprise. There was no town here yet, but Henry and Alma Gracie rode it out in their cellar. When they came up, their house was gone. Nothing left but the chimney. That's when they moved inland."

"To the place next to the park?"

"Yep. There have been Gracie's in that house for over a hundred years."

Jasper left the office and went to the counter to talk to Maisy.

"I'm going to go to the marina to see if Duke has heard anything from any of the boat owners or the fishermen."

"Okay, honey."

Jasper smiled. "I'll be back in a while."

He would've liked to walk the half-mile to the marina, but he took the Bronco. If he got a call, he wanted to be prepared. He parked in the lot, then entered the Harbor Master's office. Duke was at his desk on the phone. He looked at Jasper and raised a finger, then finished his call.

"Hey, Chief."

"Duke. I wanted to check in with you about the storm. Figured you might have some inside information."

"I have a lot of rumors and speculation."

"Let's hear it. I'll take speculation from the men who spend hours a day on the water over some guy in a suit with computerized projections and weather maps."

Duke smiled. "Word is, it's going to change direction. Some of the men say they can tell by how the wind feels and the way the waves are coming in."

Jasper nodded. "I noticed that this morning."

"What's the weather service say?"

"They still have it moving southwest, but it's slowing down. That's what Emilio did."

"Yeah. Then it changed directions several times."

"I know. I was right in the middle of it."

"Along with my boat."

Jasper laughed. "Fortunately for you, the chief decided not to report my off-the-book activities, and you got reimbursed by the department."

Duke nodded. "I would've gotten my money one way or another, Jasper."

"I'm sure you would've." He took a couple of steps back. "Keep your ears open and call me if you hear anything you think I should know about."

"Sure thing, Chief."

Jasper left the office and walked down the pier to check the water again. He rubbed his right shoulder as he studied the waves coming in. After three dislocations and surgery to put it back together, Jasper's shoulder still gave him trouble when it rained. He looked at the blue sky, then at the horizon. He wasn't sure what was coming, but his shoulder was telling him it was going to get wet.

When he heard someone behind him, he turned to see Lewis approaching.

"What do you think, Chief? Is Isabella going to tease us with her outer rim?"

"I hope that's all she's got in store for us."

Lewis looked at him. "Is your weather spidy sense kicking in?"

"I'm not sure. Do you want to take a drive to Half-Moon Bay? I'd like to get a look at the open water."

"Sure. I'm always up for any excuse that interrupts scraping barnacles."

"Let's go."

They left town and drove along an unmaintained road running along the beach and leading to the east side of the island. Half-Moon Bay was a small inlet with a usable pier and not much else. It was also the sight of Henry Gracie's first house until it was destroyed.

Jasper had to put the Bronco into four-wheel-drive for the last mile, and as they came over a rise, they could see the old stone chimney. Jasper parked near the overgrown foundation, and he and Lewis walked to the end of the pier.

The swell was much more obvious from this point, as the waves were coming in from the open water.

Lewis looked at Jasper. "What do you think?"

"The waves usually come straight in. But they're angling northwest."

"And what's that mean?"

"I'm not sure."

"Take a wild guess."

"The waves are being affected by the winds coming off of Isabella."

"I thought Isabella was headed southwest."

"I need to get back to town and check the report. I believe Isabella is thinking about paying us a visit."

"Shit. That's bad, right?"

"Yeah. That's bad."

"Anything I can do?"

Jasper headed for the Bronco. "It might be a good idea to pack up anything you don't want to lose."

"Are you serious?"

"Call it a wild hunch. Your house is surrounded on three sides during high tide. Think about what ten to twenty feet of storm surge will do."

"Am I going to lose my house?"

Jasper shrugged. "I hope to God I'm wrong."

Jasper dropped Lewis off at the marina, then returned to the station. When he came through the door, Quinn came out of his office.

"Hey, Chief. Come take a look."

Jasper followed Quinn into the office and looked at the report pulled up on the screen.

"Can't beat sailor's intuition."

"Excuse me, sir?"

"Isabella is coming for us."

"How bad?"

"Too soon to tell. But that's quite a change in direction in a couple of hours." He looked at Quinn. "Are you having lunch with Amy today?"

"I was planning on it."

"When you go to the clinic, tell Dr. Hannigan to prepare for a possible landfall from Isabella."

"Okay."

"And before you go, print copies of this latest report and post it at the usual spots around town."

Jasper went to his office and sat behind his desk. He hoped he was wrong, but he was pretty sure he wasn't. He picked up the phone and called Poppie.

"Hello?"

"Hey, babe."

"Hi my handsome husband. You usually don't call until mid-afternoon."

"I wanted to let you know I'm a little concerned about the weather."

"Do you mean the tropical storm that isn't going to come near us?"

"I mean the hurricane that has slowed down and is heading more west than south now." He leaned back in his chair. "Keep the dogs close to the house today and don't take the boys down to the beach."

"What's going on?"

"The waves are a little crazy and the tide line will most likely be higher than normal."

"Jasper. Should I be worried?"

He didn't want her to worry, but he didn't want to keep her in the dark, either. "Not yet. It's just a precaution."

Poppie sighed. "Okay. I'll keep the boys inside and put Sam on the tether when I let the dogs out."

"Thank you. And I didn't even need to use the code word."

"If you called me Penelope right now, I'd be really worried."

Jasper smiled. "Even if it was just to say, Penelope, I love you?"

"Even so."

"How's Gracie?"

"Gracie is currently sleeping."

He stood and went to the coffee machine. "And how are you?"

"I'm glad Gracie is sleeping."

"How's your back?"

"Manageable."

Jasper returned to his desk with a cup of coffee. "Don't pick up Tucker unless you absolutely need to."

"I won't. But I'm going to tell him it came from you."

"That's fine. I'll take full responsibility."

"He almost used the toilet today."

"How close is almost?"

"We made it to the bathroom door, then he ran out of there. He knows I can't catch him anymore."

Jasper laughed. "Little monster."

"What do you want for dinner tonight?"

"I'll bring something home. You take it easy."

"It sure is nice having a mother-in-law who owns a restaurant."

"What sounds good to you? And don't say burritos."

"How about fish tacos?"

"Fish tacos it is."

Jasper spent the rest of the day catching up on paperwork, interspersed with two trips to the marina to check the water. He timed the second one to catch the fishermen coming back in. He wanted to get their take on the chances of Isabella making landfall on the island. He got various answers, ranging from a direct hit to a glancing blow. But everyone he talked to agreed they wouldn't be spared. Isabella was going to be a problem.

On his way to the Bronco, he spotted Lewis loading his truck to go home. "I don't want to be the bearer of bad news, but she's coming. Just not sure how bad it's going to be."

"Sarah is going to be heartbroken if we lose the house. She kind of hated it when she first moved in there with me. But now, it's our home. This sucks."

"If you need help moving stuff, let me know. But I highly recommend you prepare for the worst-case scenario."

"Okay. I'll go break the news to Sarah."

Jasper watched his friend leave. Lewis had moved to the island twelve years ago. And moved into the house six months later. It had sat empty for two years and was barely habitable. Lewis had slowly fixed it up and by the time he married Sarah, it was pretty nice. She'd prompted him to make it even nicer. Now, they might lose it. Or at least have to start over again.

The home Jasper lost in the fire wasn't much of a house. The tragedy was losing what he had left of Ivy. But it turned out that's what prompted him to move on. He built the new house and began living again with Poppie.

Chapter Six

"Yeah, well, I didn't exactly argue the point."

As promised, Jasper brought home fish tacos for him and Poppie, and a hamburger for Jensen. While they ate, Jasper wanted to tell Poppie about the possibility of Lewis and Sarah getting flooded if Isabella made landfall.

He glanced at Jensen, who was too invested in his burger to pay much attention, but the child had a way of tuning in at the wrong moment.

"So if Isabella drops by, there's a pretty good chance Lewis and Sarah might get…displaced."

Poppie set her taco down. "No."

"Yep."

"You've told them?"

"I talked to Lewis right before I came home. It's not looking good."

She started to get up from the table. "I need to call them."

Jasper put his hand over hers. "Finish eating first."

She looked at the boys. "Right. I'll call while they're in the bath."

After dinner, Jasper cleaned up what little mess there was while Poppie put the boys into the bath, before making her call to Lewis and Sarah.

When he was done, Jasper came to the door and watched his sons playing in the tub. Poppie was sitting next to them, lost in thought after the phone conversation.

When Jensen noticed Jasper, he smiled.

"We're having a bubble fight."

"I see that."

Poppie turned and looked at Jasper.

He raised an eyebrow. "Are you okay?"

She nodded, then scooped up some bubbles and put them on Jensen's head.

She glanced back at Jasper. "I was thinking you and I could have our own bubble fight later."

Jasper pointed a finger at her. "You were already a very bad girl last night. I think we better save the bubble fights until after Gracie is born."

Poppie stuck out her bottom lip. "You're no fun, Mr. Party Pooper."

Jensen laughed. "You said poop."

Jasper grinned. "Your mom has a potty mouth, Jensen. It's time you learned that."

Poppie stood and put her arms around Jasper's neck. "I have a potty mouth?"

Jasper whispered into his ear. "Hell, yeah."

She whispered back. "Can I at least help you change out of your uniform?"

He put a hand on his top button. "Right here in front of the kids?"

"Stop." She glanced at the boys. "They'll be in bed soon."

"I'll go walk the dogs."

"Jasper."

Jasper opened his eyes. It was still dark in the room, but the bathroom light allowed him to see Poppie sitting next to him.

"Are you okay?"

"I'm not sure. I'm bleeding."

Jasper sat up. "Shit. I knew we shouldn't have done it."

Poppie shook her head. "I'm sure that's not the problem."

"Of course it's the problem. Two nights in a row."

"I promise you, that's not what's going on?"

"I really don't think you can make that promise to me." He rubbed his face. "Do we need to go to the clinic?"

She patted his knee. "It's probably nothing. Let me call Dr. Hannigan."

Jasper watched her dial the doctor and listened to her side of the conversation. From what he could gather, it wasn't nothing.

She hung up and looked at him. "He wants me to come down. I can drive myself. You stay here with the boys."

"The hell with that. I'm taking you." He took the phone from her and dialed Lewis' number.

"Who are you calling?"

"Your brother."

Lewis answered with a sleepy, "Yeah?"

"Lewis, it's Jasper."

"Why are you calling? What's wrong?"

"I need to take Poppie to the clinic. Can you come stay with the boys?"

"What's going on? Is it the baby?"

Jasper could hear Sarah in the background. "Um. Yeah. Maybe."

Sarah came onto the line. "Jasper, put Poppie on."

Jasper handed the phone to Poppie. He was actually relieved to let her deal with the particulars. He got dressed while Poppie filled Sarah in. The call seemed to end with the promise of Lewis arriving in fifteen minutes.

Poppie hung up the phone, then went to Jasper and put her hands on his chest. "This isn't your fault."

"It sure as hell feels like my fault."

"If. And it's a big if. If that's what caused this, it's both of our faults. And mine more than yours. Last night you were asleep, and I woke you up. Tonight, well, you know how much I love watching you get undressed."

"Still. I could've shown some restraint. Fought you off. Locked myself in the boys' room."

Poppie smiled. "Let's see what the doctor says."

A few minutes later, Lewis arrived looking appropriately worried and gave Poppie a hug. "Everything's going to be okay."

"I know. This is just a precaution."

"Right. A precaution. This will mess up our whole schedule. My boys are six months older than yours. You screwed that up a little this time with the girls, but it's still supposed to be five months, not two."

"Lewis, I'm not in labor."

"Well, keep it that way."

"I promise. I'll do my best not to mess up the schedule."

"Thank you."

She smiled. "The boys should sleep another few hours. Tucker will wake up first, probably around eight. Jensen loves to sleep in. Nine or ten for him."

"I got it. Don't worry. Just go. You'll probably be back before either one of them wakes up." He looked at Jasper. "Don't look so worried. Between the four of us, this is the sixth pregnancy. We can handle anything."

"You're the one freaking out about the schedule."

"Please go."

Jasper nodded. "We'll keep in touch."

Poppie looked around the room. "There's bedding in the hall closet."

"Poppie, I'm fine. This isn't the first time I've slept on your couch."

Jasper took her arm. "Come on. Let's go."

She nodded. "Okay. See you soon."

"You'll be back before you know it."

Davis Hannigan was at the door waiting for Poppie and Jasper when they arrived and parked in front of the clinic. He lived next door and would often see patients at night in the small examination room in his house. Since he was waiting at the clinic, Jasper once more figured it wasn't nothing.

He helped Poppie out of the car and when they reached the door, Davis took her arm.

"Let's get you into a room."

Jasper followed them and stood back while the doctor helped Poppie onto the table. Davis glanced at him.

"Jasper, why don't you give us a few minutes? Go get yourself a cup of coffee. I'll be doing an ultrasound, and I'll call you back in for that."

Jasper nodded as he looked at Poppie. She gave him a smile. "Go on. I'm fine."

He left for the reception area and found a fresh pot of coffee. He poured himself a cup and sat in a chair. A few seconds later, he stood. He was too anxious to sit. He walked around the room, looked out the window, then tried to sit again. By the time Davis came to him, Jasper was pacing around the room again.

"How is she? What's going on?"

"First off, the baby sounds fine. Strong heartbeat. Moving around."

Jasper sighed. "Okay."

"But I want to do an ultrasound and take a look."

"Okay. Um..." He took a breath. "I don't know if she told you, but a couple of hours ago, we—"

Davis put a hand on Jasper's shoulder. "She did. This has nothing to do with you."

"Are you sure?"

"Yes." He poured himself a coffee and took a sip. "But now that there might be an issue, you probably should abstain until after the birth."

"Gotcha." *Now tell my wife that.*

He set his cup down. "Let's go take a look at that baby." He headed down the hall and Jasper followed him. "By the way, she said it was her idea."

"Yeah, well, I didn't exactly argue the point."

Jasper followed the doctor into another room set up for an ultrasound. Poppie was reclining on a raised bed with her head elevated. She smiled at Jasper and held out her hand. He took it in both of his, then kissed her on the forehead.

Davis prepared the ultrasound machine, and put the wand on Poppie's stomach. As he moved it around and pointed out varies parts of the baby, Jasper looked on in awe. Even after multiple ultrasounds between their three babies, Jasper was amazed at the idea Poppie had a living child inside of her. It also made him emotional, and he blinked back a couple of tears. Poppie noticed and squeezed his hand.

The doctor seemed to spend some time without saying much, but when he finished, he gave them a smile. "The baby looks great. She's exactly where she should be."

Poppie sighed. "Oh, thank goodness."

"I do have a few concerns, not with your little girl, but with the uterine wall. Even though I've delivered my fair share of babies, I'm not an OBGYN. So I'd like to make an appointment for you in Culver, for today, if possible. I don't want you to wait until Monday."

Jasper studied him for a moment. "You're worried."

"At this point, let's call it cautiously concerned. I'll call Dr. Stanton. He specializes in high risk births."

Poppie sat up. "High risk?"

"I see signs of placental abruption."

"Which means?"

"If I'm correct, it means we'll be keeping a close eye on you and you'll be on bedrest for the remainder of the pregnancy."

Jasper wanted more information. "But what does it mean?"

"It means the placenta is separating from the uterine wall. At this point, it's very small."

"And if it gets bigger?"

"Then we'd start worrying about bleeding and a C-section. But we're not there yet."

Poppie looked at Jasper and he tried to give her a reassuring smile. "Let's see what the doctor in Culver says before we panic."

Dr. Hannigan nodded. "That's right. Now you two go home, get some rest. And until we get a better idea from Dr. Stanton, you stay off your feet young lady."

Poppie nodded.

He patted her hand. "I'll call you as soon as I set up an appointment."

Jasper helped Poppie off the table. "Thanks, Doc. I'll make sure she stays in bed."

"I'll talk to you soon."

Poppie leaned heavily on Jasper as they went through the clinic and out the door. When he helped her into the Bronco, she started crying.

He hugged her. "Hey now. It's going to be okay."

"I'm sorry. I'm a little scared."

"My brave Poppie, scared? Impossible." He kissed her, then closed her door and went around to get in behind the wheel. He turned in his seat and took her hand.

Poppie wiped her eyes. "Brave?"

"You're the bravest woman I know."

She cocked her head. "You've lived on this island all your life. How many women can you possibly know?"

"Well, you're braver than ninety percent of the men, too."

She gave him a small smile. "What makes me so brave?"

"You were kidnapped by a murderer. Taken hostage on a boat in the middle of a hurricane. Then helped me keep it afloat until the storm passed."

"I didn't have much choice."

"Sure you did. You could've given up. You could've cowered down below and cried."

"I actually considered doing that. But I figured you'd never let me live it down."

Jasper grinned. "And before all that, you macraméd the man."

"Which he escaped from."

"But the bravest thing you've done. The thing that has impressed me the most, is you moved here to be with me. You left your life behind and moved to this crazy little island of mine."

She put a hand on his cheek. "I'd follow you anywhere, Chief."

He kissed her stomach. "Gracie May Goodspeed, your mama is one hell of a woman."

Poppie put a finger to his lips. "Don't swear in front of the baby."

Chapter Seven

"Is there room for a small calf in there?"

When Jasper and Poppie got home, they found Lewis on the couch with Tucker sprawled over his chest. Both were sound asleep.

Poppie whispered, "Oh my goodness."

"Shhh. Let's get you to bed, then I'll get Tucker back to his crib."

They went into the bedroom and Jasper tucked Poppie into bed. "I promise you, this is going to be okay."

She patted his knee. "I appreciate you saying that. But this is one thing you can't control, Jasper."

He kissed her forehead. "Go to sleep. I'll be in soon."

When he returned to the living room, Lewis' eyes were open. "How'd it go?"

"I'll tell you after I put this little man to bed." Jasper picked up Tucker and carried him to the boys' room and placed him in the crib. He waited a moment to make sure the baby was asleep, before kissing a sleeping Jensen and returning to Lewis.

Lewis was sitting on the couch. "So, what did the doc say?"

Jasper sat next to him on the couch. "He's worried about a placental abruption."

"I don't know what that is, but it sounds serious."

"It can be." Jasper rubbed his face. "He's sending us to a specialist tomorrow, or today, I guess, in Culver."

"Shit. Is she going to be okay?"

Jasper shrugged. "I guess worst case scenario is they take the baby early. But whatever they decide, Poppie will be on bedrest until the baby comes."

"Good luck with that."

Jasper smiled. "Yeah. I think she realizes how important it is. We'll just need to round up some help."

"Well, you got me and Sarah. Whatever you need."

"I think we're going to need a team of helpers."

"We can help with that, too." Lewis got to his feet. "You look exhausted. Go get some sleep before Tucker wakes up…" He checked his watch. "In four hours."

Jasper stood and gave Lewis a hug. "Thanks, man."

"We'll talk to you in the morning. I'm sure Sarah will want to hear every detail."

"I might need her to come stay with Poppie and the boys so I can go to work for a few hours before we head to the mainland."

"I'm sure she'll insist on it. Nine o'clock okay?"

"Let's pretend the boys are going to sleep in and make it ten."

Jasper saw Lewis to the door. When he returned to Poppie, she was already asleep, so he took off his pants and got into bed as gently as he could. She mumbled something and sighed, but didn't wake up. Jasper curled up next to her and let the emotion he'd been holding back for the last two hours go. He buried his face in her hair.

"Please, God, don't take them away from me."

Somehow, Jasper managed to fall asleep, but when Tucker's cries came through the baby monitor, he felt he'd only slept for a few minutes. But looking at the clock, he was surprised it was almost eight.

He turned the monitor off, kissed Poppie and told her to go back to sleep, before going to the boys' room. Tucker was standing in his crib crying softly and was surprised to see his father come into the room, since Poppie usually worked the early morning Tucker detail.

Jasper picked him up. "Come on, Tuck, let's not wake up your brother." He got a diaper and the baby wipes and headed for the living room. The dogs woke up and were as confused as Tucker. Jasper usually walked them at nine after he showered and dressed for work. "I know guys, but you're going to have to hold it until Sarah gets here."

He changed Tucker, then sat down with him in the rocking chair by the fireplace, which wasn't lit. It was cold in the room, and he wrapped a blanket around the two of them and rocked slowly, hoping a miracle would occur and Tucker would fall back to sleep without his bottle.

He got his wish, because the next thing he knew, Jensen was patting his arm.

"Dad?"

Jasper opened his eyes. "Hey, bud." Tucker sat up and smiled, before climbing down to the floor. Jasper checked his watch. It was nine-thirty. He took a moment to wake up. The first thing he needed to do was start a fire. He prepared the fireplace, set a match to the paper underneath the pile of kindling, and waited for it to catch.

The boys were happy and being relatively quiet, so he went to the kitchen to fix them something for breakfast.

Jensen came in and watched him for a moment. "Where's mommy?"

"Mommy's in bed."

"Is she sick?"

"Not really. She just needs to rest. So I need you to keep Tucker quiet for a few minutes while I get breakfast ready."

"Okay."

Jasper opened a single serving applesauce from the refrigerator. He then mixed a bowl of instant oatmeal and put it in the microwave.

He called to the boys. "Come eat."

They followed him to the kitchen and Jasper put Tucker into his highchair while Jensen took a seat at the table.

"Can I have extra cinnamon?"

"Please?"

Jensen nodded. "Please, extra cinnamon."

Jasper put the applesauce and a spoon on Tucker's tray. The oatmeal was done, so he added more cinnamon, and put it in front of Jensen.

"Do you want a banana?"

Jensen nodded with a mouthful of oatmeal.

Jasper cut a banana in half, gave part to Jensen, and cut the rest into pieces and put them on Tucker's tray. Figuring he might've overdone it with the fruit, he grabbed a handful of cereal, and put it next to the banana.

"Okay. Is everyone happy for a minute?" Jensen gave him a thumbs up, and Tucker smiled with a mouthful of banana. "I'll take that as a yes."

He started a pot of coffee, then checked on Poppie. She was propped up on some pillows. "How's it going out there?"

"All under control." He sat on the bed next to her. "Sarah will be here soon, so I can go to work until it's time to leave."

"The doctor hasn't called yet?"

"No. I imagine the office just opened in Culver. We should hear from him soon." When the dogs barked, he stood. "That's probably Sarah." He started out of the room.

"Hon?"

"Yeah?"

"Maybe you should put some pants on."

Jasper looked at his boxers. "Good call."

He got dressed, then found Sarah in the kitchen with the boys. She had Alice in a baby carrier strapped to her chest.

"I only left them for a minute to check on Poppie."

She smiled at him. "You are the most cautious person in the world when it comes to your family. I never worry about these kids."

"Thanks. I think."

"How's Poppie?"

"She feels fine. I think she slept. You can go say hi if you want while I drink some coffee."

She put a hand on his cheek. "I think it's going to take more than coffee to wake you up today."

"Well, it's a start, anyway."

She turned her back to him. "Help me get out of this thing." He released the buckles while she supported Alice. "It seemed like a good idea at the time, but it makes me feel like I'm pregnant again."

Jasper took the carrier from her as she pulled Alice out of it. "It's a friggin' straitjacket.

"Thank you. We'll go see Poppie, now."

She headed for the bedroom and Jasper poured himself a cup of coffee. It tasted wonderful. But like Sarah said, it'd take more than that to get him through the day.

He was on his second cup and had the boys cleaned up and set free, by the time Sarah came from the bedroom without Alice. "Sorry. Girl talk. But our droning on put Alice to sleep, so that's a plus."

"No problem. If you've got this, I need to walk the dogs and take a shower. That, along with the coffee, might give me a fighting chance."

"Go. The boys and I are fine."

Since he was in a hurry, Jasper didn't take the dogs all the way to the beach. When he brought them back inside, he went into the bedroom and smiled at Poppie. "I've got to shower and go to work." He took a clean uniform out of the closet and laid it on the end of the bed.

Poppie smiled. "Oh boy, I get to watch you get dressed."

"Well, it is one of your favorite things to do."

"Go take your shower."

After he'd been in the shower for a few minutes, he heard Poppie in the bathroom.

"Is there room for a small calf in there?"

He opened the shower door. "What are you doing out of bed?"

"I'm sure Dr. Hannigan doesn't expect me to go the next two months without taking a shower."

"You better get undressed, then."

When Poppie took off her pajamas and stepped into the shower, Jasper put his arms around her. "Hello, my sexy wife."

"I'm not sexy. Not right now."

"Of course you are. I love your pregnant body."

"The three Bs. Big butt, belly, and boobs."

Jasper laughed. "Love, love, and love."

She pointed to her side. "Even this stretch mark right here?"

He bent and kissed the almost invisible mark on her belly. "I love that, too."

"Will you wash my hair?"

"Of course."

As he started lathering her hair, Poppie sighed. "What will we do if they ever stop making lilac and jasmine shampoo?"

"I'm pretty sure we've kept them in business for the last six years."

When Jasper left the house and stepped outside, he felt a shift in the wind. He looked toward the waves hitting the beach. The interval was shorter than normal. Between the wind and the waves, he was more worried than he was yesterday. When he got in the Bronco, he called Maisy on the radio.

"Good morning, Chief. Are you running late?"

"Yeah. Slightly. Didn't get much sleep last night."

"Are the boys okay? Poppie?"

"I'll fill you in when I get there. I need to go see Mom at the Loft first."

"No rush, sweetheart. Quinn and I are fine here."

"Thanks, Maisy. Can you have him pull up the latest weather information?"

"Of course."

Jasper drove into town and parked in front of The Sailor's Loft. After ringing the bell, he went inside and found Kat in the kitchen making bread.

"Hi, honey." She stopped kneading and looked at him. "What's wrong? You look tired. Are the boys okay?"

He sat on a stool and held up a freshly baked muffin. "Can I have this?"

"Of course." She put a towel over her dough and poured him a cup of coffee. "What's going on?"

"I took Poppie to the clinic last night."

"Is the baby okay?"

"Yeah. Baby's fine. But Doc took an ultrasound and thinks he saw the beginnings of a placental abruption."

"Oh, honey."

"Yeah. Too soon to panic, though. He's making an appointment with a specialist today in Culver."

"What can I do? Do you need me to take the boys this afternoon?"

"Sarah's at the house now. Poppie's supposed to stay in bed until we see what the specialist has to say." He took a bite of the muffin. "You can call Sarah and see if she needs you to take over at some point. And I guess you should call Mark and have him work tonight."

"I'll call them both." She brushed the hair off his forehead and kissed him. "It's going to be fine."

"Yeah. I know. They could end up taking the baby early. But she's a big, healthy girl, so it should be fine." He finished the muffin and drank some coffee.

"Have you eaten anything else this morning?"

"No. Could you send something to the station?"

"Of course. What would you like?"

"Hmm. Denver omelet. Heavy on the Denver."

"I'll send it over soon."

He got to his feet and kissed her cheek. "Thanks, Mom. Love you."

"I love you more, sweetheart."

Jasper left the restaurant and drove to the sheriff's office. When he went inside, Maisy came from behind the counter and took his hand.

"What's going on?"

"I took Poppie to the clinic last night."

"Oh my goodness. Are she and the baby okay?"

"Not sure. Dr. Hannigan is setting up an appointment for us in Culver today."

"Oh, he called and asked for you to call him back."

"Okay, thanks."

"And I got the coffee going in your office. Have you eaten?"

"Mom's sending something over."

"Good."

As she headed back to her spot behind the counter, Quinn came out of his office. "Morning, Chief."

"Deputy."

"I've got the morning update loading on the computer. Do you want to come take a look?"

"Yeah. I felt a shift in the wind when I left the house."

"Does that mean something?"

"Probably."

He followed Quinn into the office, and they both stared at the computer screen as the data slowly loaded. When it finished, Jasper sat in Quinn's chair.

"Shit. That's not good."

"It still headed south."

"Yeah, but it slowed down even more, and it's curving more west than south now."

"Is it going to hit us?"

Jasper rubbed his face. "It just might."

"What do we do?"

Jasper got to his feet. "I want you and Maisy to go over evacuation plans. She can dig up the records from the last big one. I believe they used the Ice House and our basement here."

"So we'd bring everyone into town?"

"If they'll come, yeah. We can't force them. But we can strongly suggest they do."

"The last hurricane was seven years ago?"

"Emilio was a glancing blow. If this one keeps turning, we'll be right in the middle of it."

"Okay. I'll get together with Maisy."

"Post this update around town first."

"Is it time to raise the yellow flag?"

"Not yet. Let's hope the internet stays up for a while. Otherwise, we won't know what's going on."

Chapter Eight

"It's my evacuation plan. I can invite whoever I want."

Jasper entered his office and sat behind his desk before calling Dr. Hannigan. Amy, his receptionist, answered the phone. Amy was also Quinn's wife of two years.

"Dr. Hannigan's office."

"Amy, this is Jasper. Is he available?"

"He's with a patient, but he told me to tell you three o'clock with Dr. Stanton. His office is on the corner of fourth and Culver Boulevard."

"Got it."

"Take care, Jasper. I'll be thinking about you guys."

"Thanks, Amy."

Jasper hung up and leaned back in his chair. They'd need to take the two o'clock ferry. He called home and got Sarah on the phone.

"How's it going there? Are the boys behaving for you?"

"They're great. And I moved Poppie to the living room on the couch. We're all doing fine."

He picked up his cup, but it was empty. "Can I talk to her?"

"Sure."

A few moments later, Poppie came on the line. "Hey."

"How're you doing?"

"I'm fine. We're playing Mouse Trap."

"Tucker, too?"

"Sort of."

Jasper got up and went to the coffee machine. "Our appointment's at three, so I'll come pick you up around one-forty to catch the ferry at two."

"I'll be ready. Your mom called. She's going to come relieve Sarah today at four."

"Good. We'll get through this." He filled his cup and returned to the desk.

"I know."

"Okay, I've got to go."

"I'll see you soon."

Jasper took a few sips of coffee, then called James.

"Hello?"

"Dad."

"What's going on, son? Kat said there's an issue with the baby?"

"We're going to Culver for an appointment. We'll know more soon. But what I'm calling about is the damn hurricane."

"It's a hurricane now?"

"Yeah. And it's slowing down and moving in a more westerly direction."

"Headed right for us?"

Jasper rested his elbows on the desk. "Not quite, but it's a possibility."

"What do you need?"

"When the big one hit fifty some years ago, what was the plan? And did people follow it?"

"I was a kid, but I remember it well. My dad had just become chief. There were closer to five hundred people in town then. Everyone gathered in the Ice House, the school gym, and the basement of City Hall."

"I thought the school got mostly destroyed."

"It did. Lost a few people. Injured dozens."

"So, don't use the gym." He took another sip of coffee.

"The Ice House will hold a fair amount of people. And it's now withstood three hurricanes. You can put the excess in the basement below the sheriff's station. Probably thirty or so. That should cover it. Not everyone will come in. Some will insist on staying with their homes. And some will stay with family inland."

"What about the animals?"

"Cats and dogs can be housed in the basement of the feed store. They'll all need kennels, or at least the majority of them."

There wasn't much livestock on the island, but enough to cause some concern. "And horses, sheep, goats, chickens?"

"The owners will need to figure out what to do with them. For Emilio, a lot of the low-lying places brought their livestock to the park. Not a lot of shelter, but they won't drown in the surge. But the city doesn't have the resources for you to deal with them. You'll have enough to worry about."

"Okay." Maisy stepped through the doorway. "Hold on, Dad."

She came to the desk. "The calls are starting. Quinn posted the storm update."

He nodded. "I'll be right out. Dad. I've got to go. The calls are starting."

"I'll round up some men from the fire department and set up a call center. You can route the calls through to us."

He knew there was good reason to call his father. "Thanks, that'll help a lot."

"When are you headed to the mainland?"

"We're taking the two o'clock ferry."

"I'll get the phones set up and let Maisy know when we're ready to field calls."

"I'll call tonight when we get back."

"Take it easy, son." Jasper hung up the phone. He and James may have had a rocky start. Twenty-eight years' worth. But the last several years had been pretty good. Though Jasper was still getting used to the new James.

By the time Jasper was ready to leave the office, James had set up the call center in the basement. Since City Hall was the only building with internet access, they could give the callers real-time updates. That's assuming the internet continued to cooperate.

Jasper checked the national weather service webpage before he left. The hurricane was continuing to increase in severity and direction. The chances of the storm hitting them were moving out of a possibility and closing in on certainty. It was now a matter of how hard they'd get hit.

Currently, the storm was a category one, which even with a direct hit, was survivable. But a category two and above, they'd start sustaining damage from the wind and the surge. Much of the island was at sea level. The Ice House was on the beach, and was a solid cement block building with few windows and doors. The interior was also big enough to hold around two hundred people if it came to evacuation.

City Hall was built on a rise fifty feet above sea level. Not a lot, but hopefully enough to keep from flooding. It was the only brick building in town built with a basement that could be sealed off and made watertight if necessary. The structure was built during the cold war era and was designed to keep the prominent citizens of Gracie Island safe from an attack, which Jasper always thought was misguided. It wasn't a bomb shelter. And if the big one had dropped, those prominent citizens would be just as dead as those they left outside to fend for themselves. The building would, however, protect them from high winds and flooding. Which is all he needed it to do.

He went home and was greeted by the dogs and the boys. He took a minute to say hi, then left them to go to Poppie. He sat on the couch and looked at Sarah.

"Can you take the boys into the bedroom for a few minutes?"

"Sure. Come on guys. Let's go clean your room."

Poppie took Jasper's hand. "What's wrong?"

"It's looking more and more likely we're going to get hit by the hurricane."

"Oh, my gosh."

He squeezed her hand. "I'd feel a lot better if you took the boys to stay with your parents until this is over."

"Not a chance."

"Poppie."

"No. I'm not leaving you. What if I go into labor? Or they want to deliver Gracie early? I'm not having this baby without you."

"Penelope."

"Jasper. No. We're staying together."

"And what happens if you go into labor in the middle of a hurricane? Do you want to deliver on a cot in the basement of City Hall?"

"If that's where you are, yes." She cradled his face in her hands. "And how would I even get there? I'm sure driving to Boston isn't something the doctor would allow me to do."

He pulled away from her and leaned back on the couch. "I could drive you."

"You need to be here. As do I. I know you worry about us. But as long as we're together, we'll be fine."

"I wish you'd listen to me on this."

"Jasper. I don't want to be away from you. Will you be evacuating everyone?"

"To the Ice House and City Hall."

"And we'll be safe there?"

"Yeah."

"Then that's what we'll do. Please. Please don't let this become a thing. Because I've already got a thing I need to worry about." She put her hand on her stomach.

He gave her a small smile. "We better go or we'll miss the ferry."

"Are we okay?"

He kissed her. "We're perfect."

"How soon before Isabella gets here?"

"Making landfall is still not a one hundred percent certainty, but if the storm keeps on the current path, four days until it makes landfall."

He stood and helped her to her feet, then opened the boys' bedroom door.

"We're headed out."

Sarah turned to him. "Everything okay?"

"Yeah. Before you hear it from someone else, looks like we're going to get hit by the hurricane."

"How bad?"

"Not sure yet. Should have a better idea in the morning."

She walked them to the door and watched as they kissed the kids. "Call me as soon as you get home."

Poppie took her hand. "I will."

Jasper was quiet on the ferry, so Poppie let him be. She knew he wouldn't insist she leave. She also knew they'd be fine. Together, they could face anything.

The ferry was mainly for passengers, but the lower deck had room for six vehicles. They were in the Cherokee, which Willis had fixed and delivered on Wednesday.

Poppie reached for Jasper's hand. "If we get a direct hit, what's that mean for the town?"

"Emilio was a glancing blow. You were gone, but there was some damage. Mostly to the homes along the eastern shore. The town is fairly protected, being on the southwest corner of the island. But a direct hit could be pretty bad."

"What about our house?"

"We'll board it up. That's really all we can do. But having had a hand in the construction, I can say she's built strong. If any house is going to survive, ours will. I wish now I hadn't dragged my feet on Gracie's room. Not sure how that will do if it gets too bad."

"I'm pretty sure you took less time to build the whole house than you've taken to frame the addition."

He brushed some hair off her face. "I was younger. And didn't have a sexy wife to distract me."

"And you weren't chief. And you didn't have two kids."

He smiled. "Sounds like a bunch of excuses to me."

She laid her head on his shoulder. "How much damage did the big one do?"

"Pretty much flattened the town."

She took a deep breath. "Let's hope Isabella passes us by."

"They rebuilt with the next hurricane in mind. Things are a lot stronger now. Better built."

She lifted her head and looked at him. "Lewis and Sarah are on the east side."

"If there's a storm surge, which there usually is, they'll get flooded."

She shook her head. "Oh my gosh."

"Lewis has been packing stuff they don't want to lose and storing it at Sarah's folks' house."

"Sarah told me. She's really upset. But of course not showing it."

"Sarah is a trooper. As are you." The ferry slowed down. "We're almost there. We'll have time to get some food if you're hungry."

"I can't eat. But get something if you're hungry."

"I'm not hungry either. Mom sent over a Denver omelet the size of Colorado. I'm good for a while."

They had a little time to kill, so Jasper drove to a pet store and parked in the lot.

Poppie glanced at the store. "Why are we here?"

"I'm going to go buy all of their pet crates."

"For?"

"We'll evacuate the animals to the basement of the feed store. Not everyone will have a crate." He opened his door. "You stay here, please."

"Yes, sir."

"I'll be right back."

He was able to get twenty crates, and he paid for them with sheriff's department funds. There was another pet store in town, and he bought ten more.

When he got into the Cherokee, Poppie looked at him. "Who will stay with the pets?"

"The Millers. They'll keep everyone fed, watered, and pottied."

"Will we have to take our guys there?"

"I don't know. I might put them in one of the cells, so we can keep an eye on them. Might not work out. Definitely keeping Penny with us, though."

"So we'll evacuate to the station?"

"Yeah. That way, as long as the communication stays up, we'll be able to keep track of the storm."

"Can Lewis, Sarah, and the kids be there with us?"

"Of course. Along with Dr. Hannigan and his wife, Mom, Dad, Aunt Peg and Uncle Beryl. It's my evacuation plan. I can invite whoever I want."

"Sounds like a party."

"It won't be a party, but we'll be together and safe."

Chapter Nine

"Can I panic, now?"

Jasper and Poppie arrived at Dr. Stanton's office a few minutes early and went into the reception area. After checking in, they sat for a half hour before Poppie was called to a room.

Jasper took her hand. "Don't let him say anything important without me."

"I won't." She kissed him, before following the nurse through the swinging door.

Jasper leaned back in his chair. He was the only man in the room. There were three women in various stages of pregnancy, and two children. He smiled at the little girl who kept peeking at him from her mother's arms. He wished now he'd changed out of his uniform. But he was so used to wearing it. And in Gracie, everyone expected to see him in it. Here in the office of an OBGYN, it was a little out of place.

He picked up a magazine, then set it down when he realized it was a women's magazine. *No Field and Stream? Or Sport's Illustrated?* It didn't matter. He wouldn't have been interested in them, either.

When the little girl slid off her mother's lap, picked up a book, and came over to him, he glanced at her mother.

The woman smiled. "Sorry. Her dad's a cop, so she assumes all men in uniform must be friends of his."

"It's okay." The child held the book out to Jasper and climbed onto the chair next to him. "Would you like me to read this to you?"

The child nodded, and the mother held out her hand. "Come here, Annie. Leave the man alone."

Jasper glanced at her. "It's okay. Honestly, I'd love the distraction."

"Well, if you don't mind."

"Not at all." He opened the book and started reading it out loud to the little girl. When the door opened, he was halfway through the book for the second time.

A nurse looked at him. "Mr. Goodspeed?"

He closed the book and handed it to the girl, then stood and followed the nurse into an office. Poppie was there, and she held her hand out to Jasper as he sat next to her.

Dr. Stanton greeted him. "Mr. Goodspeed. Or is it officer?"

"Chief, actually, but Jasper is fine."

"Okay, Jasper. Let's get right to it. Dr. Hannigan's diagnosis was correct. There is a partial abruption." Poppie squeezed Jasper's hand as the doctor continued. "It's not an emergency yet. And since you're so far along in your pregnancy, we're going to keep a close eye on it for a week or two. If it gets worse, we'll need to deliver early. If nothing changes, we'll take the baby at thirty-four weeks."

Jasper glanced at Poppie. "And Poppie and the baby will be alright?"

"That's why we're going to monitor them closely."

She put a hand on Jasper's arm. "Will I be able to deliver her naturally?"

"We'll talk about that when the time comes. It'll depend on whether the abruption gets worse. I assume you're not going to want to come here twice a week."

"No. But we'll do what we need to."

"Of course. I have faith in Dr. Hannigan. He's been delivering babies longer than I have. So I want you to check in with him twice next week for an ultrasound. The following week, I want you to come back and see me. At that point we'll talk about delivery options.

Poppie nodded. "Okay."

Jasper leaned forward. "We do have the matter of the hurricane. It's changing course and we might get hit."

"Last I heard, it was headed further south."

"Not anymore."

The doctor leaned back in his seat. "Well, let's see how that plays out. If your clinic is impacted, you might need to come here."

"We'll know more tomorrow morning."

"Do you have relatives here in town or close by? Might be a good idea to ride it out off the island."

Poppie glanced at Jasper. "He already tried to get me to leave. But our closest relatives are in Boston. Jasper needs to stay on the island. He's the chief. Everybody depends on him to handle a crisis. I'm not leaving him."

The doctor looked at Jasper. "You have somewhere safe to evacuate to if it becomes necessary?"

"Yes. And I'll make sure Dr. Hannigan is with us."

"Okay. It's up to you. I can't make you come stay in town. And I suppose if it's headed this way, you may not be any safer here." He stood and reached his hand across the desk. Jasper stood and shook with him. "You take care. And if you need to come in next week, call my office. We'll get you in right away." He looked at Poppie. "Complete bedrest, like we talked about. That means lying down or reclining. No sitting, lifting anything over ten pounds, and limit walking to the bare minimum."

"Okay."

He looked at Jasper. "I assume you have someone to help you with your kids."

"Yes. A whole island's worth."

When they got into the Cherokee, Poppie reached for Jasper's hand. "Can I panic, now?"

He leaned over and kissed her. "I'm actually a little relieved."

"How so?"

"I was afraid he was going to send you to the hospital and deliver the baby."

"Tell me again it's going to be okay."

He squeezed her hand. "It's going to be okay."

They had to wait for the five o'clock ferry. So they got a quick bite to eat at a drive-through restaurant and sat in the marina parking lot to eat.

Jasper studied his burger. "Wow. This is really bad."

Poppie laughed. "See what you've missed living on the island? Fast food. A lot of people live on this stuff."

"I don't know about living. Slowly killing themselves, maybe."

"You're just spoiled because you grew up eating your mother's cooking."

He dropped the burger into the bag. "No, this is crap." He took hers away. "Don't eat that. We'll eat when we get home."

"Can I eat the fries?"

He tasted a French fry. "A couple. Just don't let this be your next craving. I don't want to take the ferry every day to pick up fries for you."

She put a fry in her mouth. "I promise. I'll stick to burritos. Plus, your mother's fries are much better."

He looked at her. "I would though. If you really wanted me to come get you fast food fries. I'd take the damn ferry, which I hate, and get you your fries."

"I know. Because you're so sweet."

"I am pretty sweet, aren't I?"

The ferry arrived in time and Jasper drove to the lower level. They were the only vehicle, so he pulled to the front so they could see the ocean through the windshield. Jasper didn't like being on the water and he only took the ferry when he absolutely had to. But the sky, which was still clear, was a pretty shade of pink as the sun was setting behind them.

"I'm going to go check in with Jake. I think we're close enough to the island to use his radio to get in touch with the office."

"Okay. I'm fine. I'll sit here and not eat anymore French fries."

Jasper took the bag from her. "I'll take this with me."

She pouted, then smiled and threw him a kiss. "Hurry back."

Jasper left the vehicle and went up the stairs to the main deck, dropping the fries in a waste bin on the way. They seemed to have the boat mostly to themselves, and he walked across the empty deck and took another flight of stairs to the pilot house.

Jake nodded when he came through the door. "Evening Chief. How's the missus?"

"She's okay. Just needs to take it easy until the baby comes."

"Good to hear."

"Have you gotten any updates on the storm?"

Jake handed him a printout with a recent report. It was an update from the one he'd seen before they left. "I got this in Culver right before we left the dock."

"Can I use your radio?"

"Sure."

Jasper hailed the harbor master's office and got Duke.

"Hey Chief. Are you headed back?"

"Yeah. Can you connect me to dispatch?"

"Sure thing."

A few moments later, Maisy came on the radio. "Chief?"

"Maisy, why are you still there?"

"I didn't want to leave until you got back. Quinn has been on the phones all day, so I sent him home."

"You're fielding calls?"

"No, James is still downstairs with Lance. The calls have slowed down for now."

"Can you patch me to Dad, then?"

"Of course, honey. Hold on."

James came on the line. "Jasper?"

"Hey. How's it going there?"

"We've quelled the panic a bit. But I imagine once we post the updates in the morning, it'll start all over again."

"How's it look?"

"Still turning toward us. Not looking good."

Jasper took a moment. "I'm looking at the latest report. I'm afraid I agree. I'll be there soon. Will you wait for me at the office?"

"Of course. How's Poppie and the baby?"

"Dr. Hannigan's diagnosis was correct. But we're still okay at this point. For now, the plan is to keep an eye on things, and wait and see."

"Okay. I'll see you soon."

Jasper thanked Jake, before returning to Poppie.

She'd always been able to read him. "What's going on?"

"The damn hurricane is going to hit us."

"For sure?"

"Looks like it. Hopefully, it won't be a direct hit."

When they got to the island, Jasper drove to the station, and helped Poppie out of the car, up the steps, and inside the building. Maisy came from behind the counter and hugged her.

"Sweetheart. How're you feeling?"

"I'm okay. I actually feel fine."

"Let's get you to a chair."

Jasper handed Poppie off to Maisy. "Can you take her to my office? I need to go talk to Dad."

"Of course."

Jasper headed down the stairs and found James and Lance shutting down the phone lines for the night. He shook with both men.

"Thanks for manning the phones."

Lance smiled. "I think I talked to half the town today."

James put a hand on Jasper's shoulder. "I pulled up the latest information. Come take a look."

Jasper studied the computer screen for a moment. "Shit." He looked at James. "It's headed right for us."

James nodded. "Unless a miracle happens, and it turns further north, we're going to get nailed."

"Four days?"

"Looks like it. Unless it slows down, then maybe five."

"Okay. We better get some sleep. It might be the last calm night for a while."

The three of them headed upstairs and James glanced back at Jasper. "Is Poppie with you?"

"In my office."

James entered the office and sat on the edge of the desk. He smiled at Poppie, who was sitting in Jasper's chair. "What's this I hear about that baby girl giving you some trouble?"

Poppie rubbed her stomach. "It's more my body causing trouble than this little one."

"We'll take care of you." He glanced at Jasper. "Just have to deal with this hurricane. Can you keep that baby inside long enough for that?"

"I hope so. Otherwise, we might need to change her name to Isabella."

"Don't tell me you finally named this child."

Poppie glanced at Jasper and got a nod from him. She smiled at James. "Yes. We're going to call her Gracie."

James stood and looked at Jasper. "Damn. That's a great name. Does your mother know?"

"Not yet. We came up with it last night. And we've been kind of busy ever since."

"Well, I won't tell her. I'll let you do that." He looked at Poppie again. "You best get this young lady home."

He patted Jasper on the shoulder, then left the office.

Poppie smiled and whispered, "I like the new James Goodspeed."

Jasper glanced toward the door. "It still freaks me out a little bit."

Chapter Ten

"I'm pretty sure your family isn't going to get too rowdy."

When Jasper and Poppie got home, Kat was reading to the boys on the couch. They both slid off and ran to greet their parents.

Jasper picked up Tucker before Poppie was tempted to do so. She bent and kissed Jensen.

"How're my boys?"

Jensen glanced at Kat. "We've been very good for Grandma Kat."

"Thank you."

Tucker held his arms out to Poppie. "I'm sorry, honey." She kissed him. "Mommy can't hold you right now." She turned away as she felt the tears coming, and sat by Kat.

Kat took her hand. "How'd it go?"

Jasper spoke up. "I'll put these two rascals to bed while you fill Mom in."

"I'll be in to say goodnight."

Kat squeezed her hand. "What did the doctor say?"

"Dr. Hannigan was right. It's a partial abruption."

"Oh, honey."

"They're going to keep a close eye on me and the hope is to make it to thirty-four weeks."

"Two more weeks?"

"Yeah."

"You need to do everything you can to get there. Sarah and I have a whole plan worked out. She started making phone calls today, and everyone wanted to help. You'll have someone here whenever Jasper's at work."

"Thank you."

Jasper came into the room and sat in a chair. "I think they'll go down pretty quick."

Poppie stood. "I'll go say goodnight."

Jasper watched her go, then looked at his mother. "Do I look like I'm handling this well? Because that's what I'm trying to portray."

She held out her hand, and he moved to the couch. "You don't need to be strong all the time. It's okay to be vulnerable once in a while."

He took a deep breath. "I'll be vulnerable once this hurricane has passed and our baby girl is safely delivered."

"You really need to give the poor thing a name."

Jasper smiled. "We did. We came up with it last night."

"Don't keep me in suspense!"

"Gracie May."

She closed her eyes for a minute as she considered the name, then opened them and kissed him on the cheek. "Perfect." Her eyes teared up, and she swiped at one that escaped.

"Mom. Stop. I need you to be strong for me. So I can be strong for Poppie."

She wiped her eyes. "I'm sorry. Have you eaten?"

"No. We tried. But—"

"I made the boys spaghetti. I'll warm some up for you." She stood.

"You're amazing. You spend all day cooking. Then you come here and cook for the boys. Now you're cooking for us."

She smiled. "It's what I do."

"I'll go drag Poppie out of the boys' room." He stopped at the bedroom door. Poppie was sitting on Jensen's bed, holding his favorite stuffed animal. "Hon?"

She turned and looked at him. "I know." She tucked Jensen in, before handing him the worn dog. "Sleep tight, sweetheart."

She arranged the blankets in Tucker's crib, then joined Jasper at the door, and took his hand.

He kissed her. "Come sit down. Mom's fixing us some dinner."

They returned to the couch and Poppie sat and put her legs up. "I hate being so useless."

"You're not useless. You're cooking a baby."

She put a hand on her stomach. "Gracie. As much as we'd love to see you, we need you to stay put a couple more weeks."

Jasper put his ear on her stomach. "She says, 'okay, Mom.'"

Kat came from the kitchen with a beer and a glass of water. She handed the water to Poppie.

"You need to keep up your fluids." She gave the beer to Jasper. "You, too."

Poppie suddenly remembered the printout they got from Dr. Stanton. "The picture. Can you get it out of my purse?"

Jasper handed her the purse, and she took out the ultrasound picture. "Dr. Stanton has a very fancy 3D ultrasound machine. We got this perfect picture of the baby's face." She held it out to Kat.

"Oh my goodness. How precious. When I was pregnant with Jasper, the machines weren't nearly this fancy. In fact, they told me he was a girl. I was shocked to discover he was a boy."

Jasper raised an eyebrow. "Disappointed?"

"Of course not."

He looked at the picture with Kat. "We can't figure out who she looks like."

"Poppie. She looks just like her mother."

Jasper smiled. "You're right." He looked at Poppie. "We finally got one that looks like you."

"Well, it's about time. The boys are little clones of you."

"It's the Goodspeed genes. Hard to override."

Kat smiled. "Only the wavy hair is from the Steels."

Jasper ran a hand through his hair. "You always said it was the Goodspeed curse."

She smiled. "I didn't want you blaming me for it."

"Wow. You've lied to me for thirty-six years."

"You can set the story straight with the boys. Tell them it's their great-great-grandfather Justice's fault."

"No. I'm going to tell them they got it from you."

Kat left after she served the spaghetti, and Jasper and Poppie went to bed not too much later. He needed to get some sleep while he could. The next several days were going to be rough, so he should get some sleep while he could. He slept good until Tucker woke him at seven-forty-five.

Jasper kissed Poppie, then rolled out of bed. "Go back to sleep."

"Are you going into the station soon?"

"Yeah. I need to check the weather information. Sarah's coming at eight-thirty."

"Please check in when you can and let me know about the storm."

"I will." Since Tucker was jabbering, but not crying, Jasper took the time to put on his uniform, comb his hair and brush his teeth. Then he kissed Poppie. "You be good and follow the doctor's orders."

"I will."

"Love you."

"I love you, too."

He left the room to get Tucker, who was now starting to fuss. "Okay, bud. I'm here." He took the baby from his crib and changed his diaper, then put him in a clean t-shirt and pants. "Okay. You're all dressed for the day. So no dropping food on your clean shirt."

"Food."

"Yeah. I know. Time to eat soon. Milk first. Auntie Sarah will make you some breakfast."

Jasper filled a sippy cup with milk and set Tucker down with some toys. The baby scowled at the sippy cup, then looked at Jasper.

"Yummy. Milk."

Tucker tried to hand it to him. Jasper took it and took a sip. "Mmm. Milk."

Tucker took the cup back and took a sip.

"Good boy."

He went to the kitchen and made a pot of coffee. When Sarah showed up at eight-fifteen, she had Alice and Matty with her.

Jasper gave the kids kisses. "A full house today."

"Yes, lots of fun. Lewis took Micha with him. He's helping Duke get the marina ready for the storm." She laid Alice on a blanket on the floor, while

Matty went to play with Tucker. "What's the news on the hurricane? Is it still coming for us?"

"Yes. Just not sure if it's a straight shot or a glancing blow."

"What do you think?"

"I think we're going to get hit hard."

She sighed. "Worse than Emilio?"

"Yeah. Much worse." He slipped on his jacket. "I'm going to walk the dogs, then I've got to go. I'll call in a bit and give you guys an update."

"Thanks, Jasper."

"Thank you for being here."

He picked up Penny and let the other two dogs out the door. Sam ran ahead, and Blackjack took his usual slow time. His hip seemed to be bothering him more as he got older. But other than that, he was a happy and healthy dog, so Jasper wasn't too worried about him yet.

He carried Penny to the sand, and let her go as he walked toward the incoming tide. He checked his watch. The tide line was a few feet higher than it should be at this time and the waves were coming in short and faster than normal. He looked at the sky. Currently, it was clear overhead with only a few clouds on the horizon, and the wind was blowing only a few miles per hour. If he didn't know better, he'd never guess there was a massive storm headed their way.

He gave the dogs a few minutes, then rounded them up and headed to the porch. Rather than having to say goodbye to everyone again, he let the dogs in and waved to Sarah. She nodded, and he closed the door before the kids even knew he was there.

When he got to the office, both Maisy and Quinn were there.

He stepped inside. "Dammit. I thought I'd beat at least one of you here today."

Maisy smiled. "I think we're all a little anxious to see what Isabella has in store for us."

Quinn appeared in the doorway of his office. "I started your computer. We should be able to pull up the information now."

Maisy poured Jasper some coffee, then all three of them went into Jasper's office. He sat down and connected to the site. All of them reacted to what they saw on the screen.

Jasper looked at the updated information. "Shit." He looked at Quinn. "Time to raise the yellow flag. Here and at the Loft. I'll call Duke and tell him to put his up."

"Sure thing, Chief."

Jasper looked at Maisy. "Will you call Thomas and tell him to come in? We need to talk about the evacuation plan."

"Of course." She left the office as Quinn studied the computer screen.

"Any chance it'll change direction?"

"At this point, it won't matter. There's no time for it to move enough to make any difference."

"Okay. I'll go put up the flags."

"And post the meeting time. Six o'clock should give us time to get everything lined up."

"Okay. I'm on it." He left and Jasper picked up his coffee.

"Isabella, you bitch. You better not destroy my town."

Thomas showed up twenty minutes later, and they spent the next four hours cementing plans to evacuate the town in a safe and orderly fashion. They figured a few residents would leave for the mainland. But most would stay and ride it out. Seventy-five to eighty percent of them would come in to the evacuation center. The rest would stay with their property.

Jasper took a sip from his fifth cup of coffee. "I'll stay here in the basement, with my family, Mom and Dad, Dr. and Mrs. Hannigan, Lewis, Sarah, and the kids, and a few others. I figure twenty-five max."

"Sounds good. I'll go to the Ice House. Where do you want your deputy?"

"I don't expect any trouble. But it might not be a bad idea to have him with you."

"I agree."

"I'll bring Lance, Mellie, and her son here, too. I think he and I can handle anything that might arise."

"I'm pretty sure your family isn't going to get too rowdy."

"Also, if Quinn is with you, Amy will be there. She can help with any medical issues. I know it's selfish of me to keep the doc here, but with Poppie's situation—"

"Don't give it a second thought. Of course, he needs to be here to keep an eye on her."

"Thanks."

Thomas got to his feet. "I'll get Maisy to gather some help to set up the Ice House. Tonight at the meeting we'll ask for volunteers to supply food, water, and such."

"Okay. I'm going to take a drive out Lighthouse Road and let Bo and Jack know what's going on."

"Do you think they'll come in?"

"Probably not. But they should know they have an option." He stood. "I'll bring some supplies with me, in case they want to stay."

Thomas shook Jasper's hand. "We'll be as prepared as we can be. The rest is up to God."

"Let's hope nobody here has pissed Him off too bad."

Thomas laughed. "If I don't see you before, I'll see you at the meeting."

Chapter Eleven

"This was a lot easier when you guys weren't so big."

Jasper tossed two cases of bottled water in the back of the Bronco, before heading out of town. But before going to Lighthouse Road, he stopped by his house. He went inside and was enthusiastically greeted by all the kids and the dogs.

Poppie laughed from the couch. "My goodness. I never get that kind of greeting."

"That's because you don't bring grandma's cookies." The kids squealed and Jasper handed the cookies to Sarah. "I'll let you deal with these."

"Like I have any choice other than giving them to them right now."

Jasper went to Poppie. "How're my two girls?"

"We're fine. Staying put as ordered."

He kissed her and then her stomach. "Good."

"Are you home for a while?"

"No. I'm headed out to let Bo and Jack know what's coming." He lowered his voice. "I thought I'd take the two older boys with me. They love the lighthouse."

Poppie glanced at Sarah, who'd joined them, and heard Jasper.

She smiled. "Sounds like a great plan to me. I'll get them ready."

Poppie took Jasper's hand. "So, how bad is it?"

"Bad."

"So we'll be evacuating?"

"Yes. We raised the emergency meeting flags today. The meeting's at six." He patted her hand. "You don't need to be there. Neither do the kids."

Sarah returned to the couch. "They don't need to be where?"

"At the emergency meeting tonight."

"I agree. We'll stay here with the kids. Lewis can fill me in."

Jasper nodded, then smiled at Jensen and Micha. "Are you two ready to take a ride to the lighthouse?"

After getting an enthusiastic response, he took the boys outside and buckled them into the Bronco.

He took Lighthouse road every Saturday to check on the two families who lived along it. They were too far out for phone service, so Jasper was their main source of information. Both couples liked their privacy and only came into town once or twice a month. Today, though, he was bringing them bad news.

The road ended at the lighthouse, which was taken care of by Jack Anderson. He lived there with his wife, Bindi. Halfway to the lighthouse was a road leading to Bo Redford's place. He and his wife Emily lived there with three horses, a half-dozen goats and a flock of chickens.

Jasper pulled in front of Bo's place and tooted his horn before getting out. He set the boys free, and they ran to see the horses and goats.

"Stay close and don't pet them. Just look."

A few seconds later, Bo came onto his porch. "Chief. Are you here to tell me that storms headed our way?"

"Have you been to town?"

"No, but my chickens stopped laying a couple days ago, and the horses have been nervous as hell. What's going on?"

"It's a hurricane now, and it's coming for us."

Emily came out the door. "Afternoon, Chief. Can I get you some coffee?" She spotted the boys. "Or something for the boys?"

"No, thanks."

Bo came down the steps. "Are you sure about the storm?"

"We're going to get hit head on. Current winds around it are pushing one-fifty."

"Damn."

"Yeah. I wanted to give you a heads up."

"Well, shit. When do you figure it'll make landfall?"

"Monday afternoon or evening. Unless something changes. I wanted to give you the evacuation plan."

"Not interested. I appreciate the warning. But we're not going anywhere."

"I figured as much."

Bo glanced at the house. "We have a pretty good sized root cellar. We'll ride it out there."

Jasper looked at the animals. "What will you do with your animals?"

Bo studied the horses for a moment. "Not sure. I guess if it's as bad as you say, I might have to let them loose to fend for themselves. If I leave them penned up, they'll panic. And their lean-to isn't built to withstand those winds."

"Sorry. I wish I had a solution for you. But we're not really equipped to handle livestock in town."

"It's not your problem, Chief. We still might lose them. But at least they have a fighting chance to run for cover. And they can't go too far. We'll round them up when it's over."

"Okay. If you need to come into town for supplies, you'll be okay tomorrow. But after that, I'd hunker down. Looks like it'll make landfall late Monday afternoon or evening."

"Okay. We'll get ready."

"I've got a case of water with me if you want it."

"I guess we'd better take it. Thanks."

Jasper opened the back of the Bronco and took out the water. "You're far enough inland that your well water should stay clear. But don't take any chances. I'll come back as soon as I can and see how you fared."

Bo took the case of water and set it on the porch, then shook Jasper's hand. "You take care, now."

"You too, Bo." He looked at the boys. "Come on guys. Let's go."

Jensen and Micha ran to the Bronco and Jasper buckled them in. Before he got in behind the wheel, he nodded to Bo. "See you soon."

He headed down the private road for a half-mile, then turned onto Lighthouse Road. They traveled about a mile when he felt a tire blow.

"Dammit."

"Dad!"

"Sorry, honey." He pulled to the side of the road. "You two stay put." He got out and looked at the rear tire. "What are the chances of getting two flat tires in three days on each of your vehicles?" He sighed. "Shit."

He opened the door to the backseat and looked at the boys. "I'm going to let you out while I fix the tire. But you need to stay close. If I look up and don't see you, you're in big trouble."

"Okay, Dad."

Micha nodded. "Okay, Uncle Jasper."

"Good." He unbuckled them and helped them out of the Bronco. "Stay right here on the road. Don't go into the brush."

No one traveled the road, except for him every Saturday. And if someone came along, he'd hear them before they got close. He took the spare tire and the jack from the back of the Bronco and began changing the tire. While he worked on it, he remembered the last time he was broken down on Lighthouse Road. It was a few days after he first met Poppie, and he hadn't quite figured out what to make of her. He'd pretty much forced her to take the drive with him just to mess with her. Of course, he didn't expect the day to end with an escaped prisoner, a dislocated shoulder, and a disabled Jeep. But Poppie was a trooper. She hung in there and they made it back to town in relatively good shape by borrowing two of Bo's horses.

It took him about twenty minutes to change the tire, and the boys stayed in view the whole time. To them, it was an adventure. To Jasper, it was a pain in the ass. He finished and threw the spent tire and the jack into the back of the Bronco, then got the kids into the car.

"Okay. Just a slight delay. We're on our way, again."

Jensen clapped. "To the lighthouse?"

"Yes. To the lighthouse."

"Can we go inside?"

"We'll go to the top. But we can't stay too long. We need to get back to town soon."

They continued down the road until they came to a rise. When they reached the top of it, they could see the lighthouse in the distance.

"There it is."

He drove on, and a half-mile later, pulled in front of Jack's house. Both he and his wife, Bindi, were on the porch.

Jack met Jasper as he opened the door to the Bronco.

"Wasn't sure if you'd be out today. How bad is it going to be?"

"Let me get the kids." He got Jensen and Micha out of the backseat. "Stay where I can see you." The boys ran off and Jasper looked at Jack. "It's coming. Looks like a direct hit."

Jack nodded. "I noticed the change in the waves. I figured as much."

"Everyone who wants to, is evacuating to the Ice House."

Jack glanced at Bindi. "We'll stay here. It'll take more than a hurricane to knock down our stone house."

The original lighthouse was partially destroyed by the last big hurricane. It was rebuilt with reinforced stone and mortar. The house was built at the same time. But they'd get the full force of the hurricane as it came onto land.

"Are you sure?"

"I'm sure. We've got a basement."

"If you need to make a trip to town before it hits, make it tomorrow."

"We're fine."

"I brought some water if you want it."

"Save it for the evacuation center. We're okay."

"Okay, Jack. I'll come check on you early next week as soon as I can travel the roads."

"You take care of you and yours first. Don't you worry about us."

Jasper shook Jack's hand. "You take care."

"Are you going to take the boys into the lighthouse?"

"Yeah. I thought I might. I wouldn't mind getting a look at the ocean from up there, too."

Jasper gathered the boys, and they headed for the lighthouse. Being five-and-a-half and six, he wasn't sure how far they'd make it before they started getting tired.

Jensen made it about a third of the way and Jasper knelt so Jensen could get onto his back. When Micha slowed down after ten more steps, they stopped to rest. With Jensen on his back and holding Micha's hand, they continued on to the top.

"This was a lot easier when you guys weren't so big."

They ran to the windows and raised up on their toes to see through the glass. Jasper dragged a bench over and put it in front of the window for them, then took a look at the water. The wind was still calm, but the swell was now eight or nine feet and coming in faster than earlier in the day. The clouds he saw this morning had passed, and the horizon was clear. It continued to amaze him that aside from the change in the waves, there was no indication of the impending danger.

He gave the boys twenty minutes to run around and climb up and down the bench a dozen times before he told them it was time to leave. They complained a little, but then got excited about the prospect of going down all the stairs.

They made it to the bottom without anyone falling or needing to be carried, then said goodbye to Jack and Bindi before getting into the Bronco.

They got back to town in time for Jasper to drop off the boys and eat a quick meal before he had to return to town for the meeting. Kat had come to relieve Sarah again, and she made them dinner. Jasper took his plate into the living room to eat with Poppie.

She watched him for a moment. "Are they coming into town?"

"No. I hope they'll be okay."

"You did what you could. It's their choice."

"I know. That won't make me feel any better if something happens to any of them."

"I wish you didn't have to go back to town. I miss you."

"I wish I didn't have to go back into town, too. Hopefully, I won't be too late." He wasn't hungry, but he ate anyway, and when he finished, he took his and Poppie's dishes to the kitchen. Kat took them from him, then gave him a hug.

"I know you feel responsible for everyone in town. But you can only do so much."

"I know."

"And you have lots of help. So don't try to do everything yourself."

"I won't. I've actually learned how to delegate." He grinned at her. "A little bit, anyway."

"Okay. I'll see you in town. Sarah's coming back with the kids, so Lewis can go to the meeting."

He kissed her cheek. "See you there, Mom."

Chapter Twelve

"Right down to those damn little knobs you put on the kitchen cabinets."

Jasper got to the Ice House early, but the room was already starting to fill. He figured anyone able to come would be there. Jasper looked at the concerned faces of the townspeople as Thomas and Quinn came up to greet him.

Quinn glanced around the room. "How do you think this is going to go?"

"I have no idea."

Thomas put a hand on Jasper's shoulder. "I'll let you run this thing. You have the information."

"Okay." He took a breath. "I might need you to help with the Q and A at the end, though."

"No problem."

A few minutes before six, Jasper tapped on the microphone. "We're about to get started. If everyone can take their seats, please."

It took a few more minutes for everyone to settle down. But once they did, the room was dead silent. Jasper gripped the sides of the podium and took a deep breath.

"We have a lot to go over, so I want to save the questions for the end. I know there will be quite a few and we'll answer them as best we can. But let me give you all the details first."

The crowd murmured in agreement.

"I'm sure most of you have seen the updated posts on Hurricane Isabella. It's headed directly for us and will make landfall Monday afternoon. If it slows down, then early Tuesday. But at its current speed, we're looking at Monday." He gave them a minute to let the news sink in. "If you want to evacuate to the mainland, the last ferry will go out tomorrow at noon. Jake will be leaving the boat in the harbor at Culver, which is more protected than ours. He'll return as soon as it's safe to do so. He'll make an eight and a ten am run, too, so if you're going to leave, you've got three chances to do it."

Someone raised their hand, then put it back down. "We'll be setting up evacuation centers here and at city hall. Most of you will come here. Only a few of us will be at the station, and they know who they are. I'll be there relaying information to the mayor and Deputy Greyson as long as I can. But I expect the internet to be the first thing to go."

Jasper took a moment to have a drink of water. "You can evacuate your pets to the feed store. The Millers will stay there in the basement with them and make sure they're taken care of. If you don't have a crate, I bought a bunch of them and they'll be available to use. We'll be set up here by mid-afternoon tomorrow, and I encourage you all to get here and get settled in. The wind will start picking up and you're going to want to be here and settled in by nightfall. So if you haven't boarded your place up yet, get it done first thing in the morning."

He drank some more water. "I can't and won't make anyone evacuate, but I strongly suggest you do. We'll make room for a box or two of belongings, but only bring what's important. Paperwork, medication, a few mementos. Mark your boxes so you can find them again when this is all over. The Loft, the café, and the grocery store are all donating non-perishables to eat while we're here. But if you can bring anything to share with the community, it'd be appreciated. If you have children, bring what they need. Diapers, formula, and such. We'll have bottled water here, and the gas stove in the kitchen will work even after the power goes." He took a breath, and took a moment to think about if he'd forgotten anything.

"I guess that's about it." He held up his hands as the crowd started getting loud. "Hold on. Before questions, I just want to say, we'll get through this. We're Gracie Islanders. Together, we can get through anything. Okay. Let's get to the questions."

The room exploded with noise, and it didn't take long for Jasper to wave Thomas and Quinn up to the front. He held up his hands, but when the people didn't quiet down, he whistled loudly and got their attention.

"Folks let's try this in a little more organized fashion. The three of us will split up. Let's break into three groups and maybe we'll get through this a little faster.

James came up to the front of the room. "I can take a group, too."

The crowd seemed agreeable and the four men each took a corner of the room with the people dividing pretty evenly between them. But even doing it that way, they were still there for almost two more hours. By the time the crowd dispersed, it was after nine. Then Jasper, Thomas, Quinn, and James stayed for another hour, making sure they'd covered all their bases.

Jasper finally got home at ten-thirty and everyone was asleep. Sarah left at nine once she was sure the boys were down for the night. He took the dogs for a quick run, then sat at the kitchen table with a glass of water. He was surprised when Poppie came in and sat across the table from him.

He took her hand. "You are a very welcome sight."

"Was it bad?"

"Just long and stressful. As you can imagine, everyone is in panic mode. I feel like I answered the same dozen questions over and over again."

"How many do you think will evacuate?"

"More than I originally thought. I'd say ninety percent."

"Good." She squeezed his hand. "I want you to promise me something."

"Anything."

"If we need to rebuild. I don't want you to change a thing. I love this house. I love that you built it. And it's where I want to grow old with you and sit on the porch and watch our grandchildren play."

He smiled. "The first time you said that to me, it seemed like it was so far away. But now that I've seen how fast time has flown once Jensen was born, it doesn't seem that far off."

"Everything the same?"

"Right down to those damn little knobs you put on the kitchen cabinets."

"Thank you."

He kissed her hand. "But we're going to stay positive and not worry about the house. We have enough other stuff to worry about. Like keeping you and the kids safe."

"Okay."

He stood and helped her to her feet. "How about a nice long shower?"

"In case it's our last one for a while?"

"Penelope."

"Sorry. Sounds wonderful."

They took a long shower and Poppie tried not to get emotional. But she knew how devastated Jasper would be if they lost the house. He already lost the first house he lived in with Ivy to the fire. But this one, he designed and built. This one he had their children in. It'd be very hard on him.

He seemed to know what she was thinking, and he put his hands on her face. "Hey. We're going to be fine."

She leaned into him as best she could, with Gracie in the way. "I know."

"I'd be happy living in Dad's old camp trailer with you and the kids. As long as we're together, nothing else matters."

He'd lived in James' trailer for almost ten months while the new house was being built. It was now back on James' property and most likely wouldn't survive the hurricane.

When they settled into bed, Jasper was restless. She snuggled into him. "You really should try to get some sleep. It might be the last night of sleep you get for a few days."

He sighed. "I'm trying."

"What can I do?"

"Talk to me."

"Are you saying I'll bore you asleep?"

He laughed. "No. The sound of your voice is soothing. It'll lull me to sleep."

Poppie started telling him about her day, slowly and in great detail. After about five minutes, she felt him relax. A few minutes after that, he was asleep. She kissed him, rolled onto her side, and fell asleep.

The sound of the phone ringing woke Jasper. He fumbled for the receiver and picked it up.

"Chief Goodspeed."

"Jasper, it's Lewis."

Jasper sat up. "What's wrong?"

"Sarah and the kids and I are on our way over. We're two hours away from high tide and the water is on the porch already."

"Shit."

"Yeah. Can you put us up for the night?"

"Of course. I'll meet you out front."

Poppie put a hand on his back. "What's wrong with Lewis?"

"His house is about to flood. They're on the way over."

"Oh my gosh."

Jasper kissed her. "I'm going to go help them get settled. I'll send Sarah in to talk to you."

He got dressed, before going into the living room. When he saw headlights pulling into the driveway, he went onto the porch. The wind had picked up, and the temperature had dropped. The rain would start soon.

Lewis got out of the car, and opened the backseat door. He took out Micha and handed him to Jasper, who'd come off the porch. Lewis then got Matty while Sarah got Alice. They all went into the house.

Jasper rubbed Micha's back. "You can put these guys in with the boys. There's a port-a-crib in the closet for Alice." He took Micha and put him in bed with Jensen, while Lewis put Matty in Tucker's crib. Then the two men setup the port-a-crib for Alice.

Once everyone was settled in, they went to the living room.

Sarah hugged Jasper. "Thank you. I'm going to go see Poppie."

Jasper nodded, then looked at Lewis. "You want to go check the tideline with me?"

"Yeah."

Jasper put on his coat and picked up the flashlight, then went outside with Lewis. As they stepped off the porch, Lewis shook his head.

"I figured we'd probably get flooded. But not this soon. If we're taking on water now, before it even gets here, we're screwed."

Jasper put a hand on his shoulder. "I'm sorry, man. Did you prepare as much as you could?"

"We got everything off the floor. But a lot of damn good it'll do if the water's three or four feet high."

"We can go over at daylight and see if there is anything more we can do."

"Thanks. I'd like to do that."

"Of course." Jasper stopped walking when he saw the tide line in front of him. It was about ten feet higher than normal.

Lewis glanced back at the house. "You better sandbag the doors before you leave tomorrow."

"This sucks, man."

"No shit."

When the men returned to the house, Sarah had put a bed together for her and Lewis on the couch. Jasper said goodnight to them, then went in to Poppie.

He got undressed again and got into bed next to her.

She held his hand. "How high is the water?"

"It has a way to go before it gets to the house. I'll board it up in the morning and we'll sandbag it before we head into town." He kissed her. "I think we're high enough to stay dry."

"What about Lewis and Sarah's house?"

"They're going to take on water. It's just a matter of how much. Lewis and I are going over in the morning to see if we can do anything. Move stuff out. Whatever."

"Okay. Please try to get some sleep."

"Yeah. Probably not going to happen."

Chapter Thirteen

"It'll still be here when we come back."

When Jasper drove Lewis to his house, they needed to park down the road. He stopped the Bronco thirty feet from the water. It wasn't too deep yet, but small waves were coming in every few seconds and the wind was picking up, which would soon create whitecaps. They got out and looked at the house. The water had covered the porch and was right below the windowsills.

Lewis shook his head. "No sense going any further."

"We can wade over there. Bring some stuff out."

"We packed and moved out what we really needed and wanted. There's nothing more we can do."

Jasper put a hand on Lewis' shoulder. "I'm sorry, man."

"Let's go."

Lewis was quiet on the way back and Jasper didn't try to talk to him. He knew what it was like to lose everything.

When they got back to the house, Lewis got out of the Bronco. "Let me go talk to Sarah for a minute, then I'll come help you get the windows boarded up."

"Take your time. I'll haul the plywood out of the shed."

On Gracie Island, every house had enough plywood sheets, cut to size to cover their windows. Even though they'd been lucky up to now with hurricanes, they had a severe enough storm every couple of winters to warrant protecting the windows from the wind.

Jasper brought the boards out and leaned them against the house, along with some two-by-fours to secure them to the window frame. Next he got two hammers and a can of nails. This was the third time in five years he had to board up the house. But this was by far the worst storm. He looked at the house. "You better still be here when we come back."

Lewis came around the corner. "She will be. Otherwise, Sarah and the kids and I will have to go live with her parents."

Jasper laughed. "You like Sarah's parents."

"Yeah. But I like you more."

Jasper looked at the framed in room he'd been building for Gracie. It was supposed to be done by now. It was completely framed in, with plywood on the roof and the floor. He hadn't yet made the opening in the adjoining wall, which now he was glad about.

Lewis came up beside him. "Don't worry about it. Most likely, I'll be here to help you rebuild it."

Jasper nodded. "I'll let you build it all. Earn your keep."

"You're the house builder. I just maintain boats. I live to scrape hulls."

It took two hours to get the windows covered, along with the three French doors around the back deck and the skylight. While they were doing that, the women were getting the kids ready to evacuate. Each child was allowed to bring two toys, their favorite blanket, and a pillow. Sarah packed a couple of sets of clothes for the boys and helped Poppie pack some things for her and Jasper. Despite how thrifty they were trying to be, they still ended up with a good sized pile by the front door.

As the house got darker with each window covering, the kids thought it was a great adventure and wanted the lights off so they could play hide-and-seek with flashlights. They got rowdy, but the women let them have their fun. Soon enough, they'd be cooped up in the basement of the sheriff's station.

It started raining as Jasper and Lewis were boarding the last window. The wind had already increased, making the job more difficult. Holding a sheet of plywood in a thirty-mile-per-hour wind wasn't an easy task.

By the time they came inside, they were wet and worn out.

Sarah kissed Lewis. "Do you want to change into dry clothes?"

"We're just going to get wet again loading the vehicles."

"I'd love to have a beer though, while the power is still on and they're cold." He looked at Sarah. "I know it's not even noon yet. But today calls for an early beer."

Jasper came up beside him. "I completely agree." He peered into the dark house. "Where's my wife?"

"I'm over here."

Jasper took two beers from the refrigerator and handed one to Lewis. Then sat on the coffee table in front of Poppie.

"Are you soaked?"

"Pretty much, yeah."

"You should change."

"Like Lewis said, we're just going to get wet again. I'll change once we get to the station."

"When should we go?"

"As soon as you're ready. And after I drink this beer. I know it's early yet, but I need to be there when people start arriving. And I want to get you settled in."

"What about the dogs?"

He sighed. "As much as I hate to do it, I'll take Blackjack and Sam to the feed store. But Penny's coming with us."

"Good. She's a little nervous with the wind and the hammering."

Jasper whistled and all three dogs came to him. "I just wanted Penny." He patted Blackjack and Sam, before picking up Penny. She was shivering, and he handed her to Poppie. "You're fine, girl. I promise you, we'll keep you safe." Penny snuggled into the blankets. "Are you guys ready?"

"I think so. We ended up with quite a bit of stuff. But there are nine of us."

"It's fine." He stood and kissed her. "Did you get my guitar?"

"Of course."

"Lewis and I will load the Bronco and the Cherokee. I want both vehicles in town.

The men loaded the bags and put the kids into the Cherokee and Lewis' SUV. Jasper then put the dogs into the Bronco. With Sarah driving the Cherokee, Lewis in his vehicle, and Jasper and Poppie taking the Bronco, they convoyed into town.

As they pulled away from the house, Jasper saw Poppie start to tear up. He took her hand. "It'll still be here when we come back."

"I hope so."

Jasper drove down the driveway, and with one last look at the house, he pulled onto the road.

They made it into town and parked the vehicles on the leeward side of the station. Once they got Poppie, Sarah, and the kids inside, Jasper and

Lewis unloaded and took their things to his office. Later on, they could figure out what they would need downstairs.

Jasper made a pot of coffee to try to warm up from the inside, then called Kat.

"Hello?"

"Hi, Mom. Do you and Dad need any help?"

"No honey. Your father got the house boarded up. Then he, Beryl, and Mark secured the Loft. Are you still at home?"

"No. I brought everybody in. Lewis and Sarah. All the kids. I need to take the dogs to the feed store. Then I'll be here unless I need to be somewhere else."

"We'll be there soon. Maisy and Thomas are at the Ice House and she said people are starting to come in."

"Okay. I'll see you soon."

He headed downstairs to see what everyone was up to. Sarah had built a nice little nest for Poppie in the larger cell. And Poppie and Penny were settled in. The kids were running around the open space, again making too much noise, but no one wanted to calm them down yet.

"I'm going to take the dogs to the feed store. Anybody need any last-minute items? Everybody is probably closed. But I can try."

Sarah looked around. "I think we're all fine. What can we do here?"

"Start setting up the beds. Mom will be here soon with a bunch of food. Mellie and Lance are bringing water and ice. Hopefully a sixpack or two of beer."

Lewis grinned. "We'll get started."

"Okay. I'll be back soon."

As he went upstairs to the lobby, Dr. Hannigan and his wife came through the front door. The doctor had his arms full of stuff and he set it down inside the door. Jasper shook his hand.

"Do you have more to bring in?"

"Yes. A few more things."

"Mrs. Hannigan, you can go downstairs. Poppie, Sarah, and Lewis are down there setting things up. I'll help Doc bring in the rest of your things."

"Thank you, dear."

She headed down the stairs and Jasper and Davis went outside. It wasn't currently raining, but the wind was blowing hard. He'd parked by Jasper's vehicles, and between the two of them, they got the rest of the stuff moved inside.

Davis put a hand on Jasper's shoulder. "I want you to know I'm prepared to deliver your daughter if it comes to that."

"Do you think it's possible?"

"Possible? Yes. Probable? No. But it doesn't hurt to be prepared. It's going to be a stressful couple of days."

Jasper took a breath. "Okay. Thanks."

"Don't worry, son. I'll keep a close eye on her. There won't be any surprises."

"I ah...I need to take the dogs to the feed store."

"I'll go get set up downstairs."

Leaving the dogs was harder than Jasper thought it was going to be. They didn't understand why they were caged up, or why he was leaving them. He petted them through the wire crate.

"I'm sorry guys. But you'll be fine here. Lots of other dogs to look at."

Ted Miller came up to Jasper. "I know it's hard to leave them. But we'll take good care of them. And we'll let them out for some exercise and such."

He nodded toward the far end of the basement. "The floor is dirt down there. It'll give them a place to do their business."

Jasper shook hands with Ted. "Thanks, Ted. See you in a couple of days." He left feeling guilty. At least Penny would be with them. And Kat was bringing Pepper to the station. He was getting old and never fully recovered from the burns from the house fire. This was no place for him.

When Jasper got outside, the rain had started again. He looked up and down the street and it seemed the buildings were all as prepared as they could be to weather the storm. When he saw someone leaving the grocery store, Jasper crossed the street and went inside. Abe Steadman was manning a register and had a few customers in line.

Jasper approached him. "How much longer are you staying open?"

"This is it."

"Can I go grab something really quick?"

"Of course."

Jasper walked to the frozen food section and picked up a box of Poppie's favorite frozen burritos, and brought it to the register.

Duke was in line in front of him with a bottle of bourbon and a case of beer in his cart.

Jasper shook his head. "I hope you're not planning on bringing that to the Ice House."

Duke laughed. "No. This is all for me. I'm holing up in my Dad's old place. It has a root cellar."

"Okay. Good luck to you."

Duke held up the bottle. "Don't need it with this."

Jasper put the burritos on the counter.

Abe rang him up. "Poppie still craving these?"

"Yeah."

"I'm not sure how long my generator will work without being tended to, so those might be the last ones for a while."

"I'll tell her to make them last." He handed Abe some money. "Do you need help finishing up here?"

"No. I'm all ready to go. I'll board up the door on my way out."

"Okay." Jasper shook hands with Abe. "See you in a few days."

Jasper left the store and got into the Bronco, but instead of going back to the station, he drove toward the marina and parked near the Ice House. He greeted several people who were going inside, then looked for Thomas. He spotted Quinn first.

"Chief. Everything okay?"

"Yeah. I wanted to check in with you guys before I hunkered down. I don't know how long the phone lines will stay up."

"Things are going smoothly here. Everyone's cooperating, helping out, being neighborly."

"Good. I expect it'll stay that way. I want you to take a head count once you figure everyone has come in. I want to make sure everyone is accounted for."

"Sure thing."

"Either Dad or I will stay by the phone as long as it's working. And if the internet is still up when I get back, I'll call with a weather update."

"Okay."

Jasper put a hand on his shoulder. "Good work these last few days."

"Thank you."

Jasper smiled. "As always, of course."

Thomas came up to them. "Jasper."

"Hi Thomas. Just doing a last check in."

"We're looking good here. How's it at the station?"

"Oh, you know, those rowdy Goodspeeds. Hard to keep them under control."

Thomas smiled. "You best get back there and kick some ass."

"Yes, sir, Mayor."

Chapter Fourteen

"Go tell your wife it wasn't my idea."

While everyone was getting settled in, Jasper and James were upstairs talking with Thomas on the phone. They'd gotten a final update before the internet stopped working. If nothing changed this late in the game, the hurricane would make landfall mid-afternoon tomorrow. The winds were already forty miles per hour, with gusts over fifty. The rain squalls had started, and the tideline was fifteen feet higher than normal.

They built the Ice House with a storm surge in mind, and the foundation was a solid five feet above ground level. Even so, the water would get close and the doors had all been sandbagged.

Jasper had Thomas on the phone, but it was only a matter of time before they'd get cut off. At that point, each evacuation center was on their own until the hurricane passed.

"So, is everyone accounted for?"

"Quinn is doing a final headcount now. We expected two hundred and twenty. Hold on." He was off the line for a moment. "Jasper, looks like we're missing two people who should be here."

"Who?"

"Burt and Wilda."

"Shit. Did anyone talk to them? What about Cliff? He's Wilda's neighbor."

"He said he tried knocking on her door. She didn't answer, and it was locked. So he figured someone got her out."

"Dammit."

"Do you want me to send Quinn to her place while we still can?"

Jasper sighed. "No. I'll go." Wilda was in her seventies and had been failing both physically and mentally over the last couple of years. But she always remembered him, though she often thought he was still sixteen.

"Jasper. You should send someone else."

"If Wilda didn't answer for Cliff, it means she's scared. She'll open the door for me."

"Okay. But go now, before it gets any worse."

"I'll check on Burt, too. I saw him yesterday, and he said he'd probably come in." He took a moment. "If he doesn't want to come in...?"

"You can't force him, Jasper."

"Not even on the grounds of mental incapacity?"

"Not without a court order."

"I can't make a spur of the moment judgement call?"

"Jasper. You know how Burt is. If you try to make him do something he doesn't want to do, he gets combative. Just do what you can. If he wants to stay, make sure he has what he needs."

"Okay. Take a final headcount and make sure we're not missing anyone else. It'll take me a few minutes to get out of here. Dad will stay by the phone."

"Will do, Jasper. Be careful out there."

"I will."

James looked at him. "Thomas is right. Send Lance. Or I'll go."

"I'm not going to ask someone else to go out there. I'll be fine. And like I said. I may be the only one Wilda will answer the door for." He smiled at James. "And you, of course. She's always had her eye on the chief."

James smiled. "Not the way you're thinking. She taught English when I was in high school. She believed I had potential."

"For?"

He shook his head. "A secret I'll take to the grave."

"Dad. Come on."

James sighed. "She loved Shakespeare. Taught it every year. Turns out I had a gift for writing in iambic pentameter if you must know."

Jasper laughed. "Wow."

"Ask your mother. She knows."

"Wow, again. I'm almost sorry I made you tell me."

James headed for the stairs and Jasper followed him down, then motioned for Lewis.

Lewis joined him at the bottom of the stairs. "What's up?"

"I just learned something really weird about my dad. But I'll put that aside for now. Burt and Wilda are no shows at the Ice House."

"Well, damn."

"Yeah. I need to go see if I can bring them in."

Lewis looked at him for a moment. "I'll come with."

"No. You need to stay here with the families."

"In case you don't come back?"

"No. Of course I'm coming back. It's not too bad out there yet."

"Fine. Then I'm coming with you."

Jasper studied him for a moment. "Shit. Go tell your wife, it wasn't my idea."

Lewis left to talk to Sarah and Jasper went to Poppie. She was with the boys in the nest Sarah built for her in one of the cells. Penny was curled up on one side and Alice was asleep on the other.

As soon as she saw him, she knew something was up. "What?"

He knelt next to the bed. "I need to go out and bring in Wilda. She got left behind. I also need to check on Burt."

"Why does it need to be you?"

"You know why."

She put her hand on his cheek. "I love you feel the need to save and protect everyone. But I also hate the fact you need to save and protect everyone."

"It comes with the job."

She moved her hand to his heart. "No, it comes from here."

He kissed her. "I won't be long. And Lewis is coming with me."

"So both of the men I love are going out into the pre-hurricane weather?"

"We'll be back soon." He kissed her again. "Also, I have a juicy family story for you. But I'll save it until I get back."

"You can't leave with that."

"Sure I can." He picked up Tucker who hugged his neck.

"Pee."

Jasper shook his head. "Seriously?"

Poppie laughed. "Sarah can take him."

Jasper set Tucker down, then knelt in front of Jensen. "I need to go help someone. But I'll be right back. Be good and listen to your mother. And everyone else in here because you're related to most of them."

Jensen nodded. "Yes, Dad."

"And keep your brother occupied."

"Okay."

"Love you." Jasper got to his feet.

Poppie tilted her head. "You can't leave me hanging. At least give me a hint."

Jasper thought a moment.

"Shall I compare thee to a summer's day?
Thou art more lovely and more temperate:
Rough winds do shake the darling buds of May."

"You're related to Shakespeare?"

Jasper laughed. "No. But good guess." He left the cell and found Lewis waiting by the stairs. "How'd it go with Sarah?"

"She says if I don't come back, she'll never speak to me again."

"Sounds reasonable."

"I know. Right? I didn't dare point out her illogical logic."

"Good thinking."

James was waiting for them upstairs with coats and slickers.

"The rain is coming down pretty hard." He handed them each a flashlight. "Without power, it's going to get dark out there as soon as the sun goes down."

Jasper figured they had an hour until sundown. "I plan on being back by then." He shook James' hand. "See you soon."

"Don't take any chances. If you can't get to them…"

"I know. I need to try."

"I'll stay up here until you get back."

Jasper nodded, before opening the door. The wind and rain hit him in the face as he fought his way out the door.

Lewis followed him. "Holy crap."

Jasper yelled over the wind. "It's not too late to change your mind."

They made it to the Bronco and got inside, taking a minute to catch their breath.

Lewis grinned. "This reminds me of Emilio."

"When you came banging on my trailer door?"

"Yeah. Except it never got worse than this."

"Unfortunately, this time, it's just the beginning."

Jasper backed onto the street, which had a stream of water running down the middle of it. He wasn't sure if it was from the rain or the ocean. He put the Bronco into four-wheel-drive to give him more control and headed down the road.

"What's the quickest way to get to Burt's?"

Lewis thought for a moment. "Through the park."

"Yeah. Then we can cut through the school to get to Wilda's. That'll save us several miles."

"Sounds like a plan."

As they headed to the park, the wind was behind them, but when Jasper turned and headed across the grass, they got hit from the side.

Lewis looked at Jasper. "Are we going to flip?"

"No. It'll take more than fifty-mile-per-hour gusts to blow us over."

Lewis grabbed the handle above the door. "Okay, Chief. I'm trusting you know what you're talking about."

When Jasper veered off their straight path, Lewis looked at him. "What are you doing?"

"I want to check the gazebo."

"Why?"

"The gazebo is..."

"Special. I know. But even if it's still standing, that doesn't mean it will be tomorrow."

Jasper kept going until he could see the outline of the gazebo through the rain. At this point, it was still there.

Lewis pointed at it. "Satisfied?"

Jasper nodded.

"Can we get back to our mission now?"

Jasper turned the Bronco back to the original direction.

"So what did your dad tell you that spooked you?"

Jasper sighed.

"Shall I compare thee to a summer's day?

Thou art more lovely and more temperate:"

He glanced at Lewis who appeared confused. "Shakespeare."

"The *Romeo and Juliet* guy?"

"Yes. Did you sleep through high school English?"

"Whenever possible, yes."

"That explains a lot."

Lewis squinted at him. "Are you saying I'm stupid because I can't quote Shakespeare?"

"No. Not at all. You were smart enough to get Sarah to marry you. So, who am I to judge?"

When a metal garbage can came flying through the air and bounced off the windshield. Both men were too shocked to even swear as Jasper hit the brakes. After a moment, he looked at Lewis.

"There goes my windshield."

The can left a circle of shattered glass with several cracks coming out of it. A few yards further, they came to a downed tree. Jasper drove around it and continued on the way. When they both spotted something dark and large heading toward them, Jasper hit the brakes again.

"What the hell it that?" A moment later, a horse came running toward them, then veered at the last second and ran past. Jasper looked at Lewis. "One of Bo's horses." He started to drive again, but Lewis put a hand on his arm.

"Wait. They might be traveling together."

As soon as he said it, another horse charged by and Jasper glanced at Lewis again. "He has three."

"Give it a minute."

The third horse ran by, nearly hitting the Bronco's right fender.

Jasper peered through the windshield. "I wonder if the goats are with them?"

"They probably formed their own herd."

Jasper smiled. "Okay. Here we go." He started driving again as he thought about a goat herd running around the island looking for shelter. "I like the goats. I hope they'll be okay."

"We're not going to go rescue the goats."

When another large object appeared in front of them, this one rolling rather than running on four legs, Jasper turned the wheel to avoid it. Lewis watched out his window as the portable bathroom rolled by.

"I hope nobody was in there."

Jasper started laughing and glanced at Lewis. "I'm glad you came with me. This wouldn't be nearly as fun by myself."

"Fun? This is fun for you?"

"Flying garbage cans, charging horses, porta-potties, just another fun day on Gracie Island." They arrived at the edge of the park, and Jasper looked both ways down the street to take stock of where they were. "I can't tell for sure, but I believe Burt's place is to the left."

Lewis looked down the street through the pouring rain. "I think you're right. I can see the school gym. Maybe."

"Okay. Left it is. Then we'll shortcut through the school to Wilda's."

Chapter Fifteen

"Why am I grabbing the cat? You're the chief."

J asper parked as close as he could to the front door of Burt's small house, then he and Lewis went to the door.

Burt was in his forties, but had the mind of a child. He was self-sufficient to a degree, but the town kept an eye on him and made sure he ate and had what he needed. He lived alone in the house he grew up in with his single mother who passed ten years back.

"Burt? It's Jasper." He tried the door and found it unlocked. He opened it a few inches. "Burt, I'm coming in." Jasper opened the door and he and Lewis stepped inside. The boarded-up windows made it dark, so they turned on their flashlights. The house was sparsely furnished and surprisingly neat. There was a piano in one corner. Jasper had been told Burt was a piano prodigy. But he'd never seen it for himself.

"Burt, are you here?"

Lewis tapped Jasper's shoulder. "I'll go check the bedroom."

"Okay." Jasper headed for the kitchen. "Burt?"

Other than a few dishes in the sink, it was tidy as well. He spotted a small trapdoor in the middle of the floor and tapped it with his boot. "Burt?"

The door opened and Burt's head appeared. "Chief?"

"Yeah, Burt, it's me."

"Is it over?"

"No, it's just starting." Burt started to close the door, but Jasper stopped him. "Wait. I'm here to help. To bring you to the evacuation center."

Burt looked at Jasper's hand holding the trapdoor. "I don't want to go with you. I want to stay here."

"Are you sure?" Jasper looked at Lewis as he came up beside him. "Is that a cellar?"

Burt nodded. "I have what I need. I don't want to go. Mrs. Russell fixed me right up."

Jasper glanced at Lewis, who shrugged. "You have water and food? Blankets? Is your dog down there with you?"

"Yes. Rufus is here. He doesn't want to go either."

Jasper let go of the door. "Okay, Burt. I won't make you go. But we won't be able to come back for you if you change your mind.

"I won't change my mind." He started to close the door. "Come tell me when it's over."

"Okay. I'll come check on you as soon as I can."

Burt closed the door without responding.

Jasper looked at Lewis. "He wants to stay."

"Come on, let's go."

Jasper hesitated, not wanting to leave Burt behind.

Lewis put a hand on his back. "Jasper, the man wants to stay in his home."

Jasper nodded. "Right. Let's go."

They left the house and made a run for the Bronco. The rain had let up a little, but the wind seemed even stronger. Jasper backed onto the street, before driving between Burt's house and the neighbor's. A quarter mile down the alley, they came out in front of the school playing field.

Lewis laughed. "The principal's going to be pissed you drove across his grass."

"I'm pretty sure my tire tracks will be the least of his problems when this is all over."

Jasper eased the truck up the curb, then drove across the large expanse of grass. It was slick from the rain, and even in four-wheel-drive, the tires lost traction a few times. As they got to the other side, the chain link backstop from the ball diamond lifted off the ground, and tumbled a few times before landing.

Jasper watched it rock back and forth. "Now that, he'll be pissed about."

They drove around it, then pulled onto the street. Wilda's place was the second house down the from the school. He pulled into her drive and once more tried to park the Bronco as close as he could to her front door. One of her porch supports had been knocked off its foundation and the porch roof slanted at a sharp angle. The runoff from the rainwater caused a small waterfall. Jasper ducked under the roof and avoided the puddle at the bottom of the waterfall, before knocking on the door. When he got no answer, he tried the knob and found it locked.

"Wilda? It's Jasper Goodspeed. Come open the door." He picked up a frog sculpture next to the door and took the key from under it.

"How'd you know that was there?"

"I used to house sit for her when I was in high school." He unlocked the door, and they entered the house. "Wilda, it's Jasper. I've come to help you." He looked at Lewis. "Check the bedrooms. I think she sleeps in that one."

Lewis headed to the indicated bedroom, while Jasper went to the kitchen. He opened the pantry and found Wilda inside. She was sitting in a corner and looked scared to death.

Jasper knelt in front of her. "Wilda, are you okay?"

She looked confused, then seemed to recognize Jasper. She reached for his hand. "Jasper?"

He smiled. "Yes. I'm here to help you."

"The storm is so bad. I didn't know what to do."

"It's going to get worse. I need to take you somewhere safe."

"But my house?"

"Wilda, you're not safe here. Will you come with me?"

"Where?" Lewis came up behind Jasper and she grabbed Jasper's hand. "Who's that?"

Jasper glanced over his shoulder. "That's Lewis. He's my friend. He's here to help, too."

"I don't know Lewis."

"You know Sarah? She plays the organ at church on Sundays."

"Sarah? Yes. I know her. Such a pretty thing. And darling children."

"Lewis is Sarah's husband."

Wilda frowned at Lewis. "You don't come to church."

"No ma'am I don't."

She let Jasper help her to her feet. "Where are we going?"

"We're going to take you to the station. We're evacuating in the basement. The chief is there. And Kat and Peg."

"Oh, okay. They're my friends."

"Dr. and Mrs. Hannigan are there, too. We'll all be safe until the storm passes. Do you need anything? Do you have medication you take?"

She thought for a moment. "It's all in my purse. Dr. Hannigan told me to keep it all together in case we evacuate, but no one came. I didn't know what to do."

"We're here for you now. I'm sorry I didn't come sooner."

"It's okay, Jasper. You have a lot to worry about. Is the chief at the shelter, too?"

Jasper glanced at Lewis. "Yes, ma'am. The chief will be there."

In Wilda's mind, James was still chief and Jasper was the teenage boy who used to come work in her yard during the summer.

"We'll bring your purse." He looked at Lewis.

"Right. Purse patrol." He left to find Wilda's purse.

Wilda followed Jasper out of the pantry and he helped her put on a coat hanging from the back of the door. A few moments later, Lewis returned with Wilda's purse and a blanket. Jasper took the blanket and wrapped it around Wilda.

"This will keep the rain off of you. I'm going to carry you to the car. Is that okay? It's really windy out there."

"You're such a good boy. How's your mother?"

"She's fine. She'll be happy to see you at the shelter. But we need to go now."

She nodded, then stopped walking. "Mr. Barnabas."

"Who?"

"My cat. I can't leave my cat."

Jasper looked at Lewis. "Have you seen a cat?"

Lewis shook his head.

"Wilda, where would Mr. Barnabas go if he was scared?"

"Under my bed."

Jasper took Wilda to a chair. "Okay, sit for a moment. We'll get the cat. Do you have a carrier for him?"

"In the hall closet." Something crashed against the house and she jumped and grabbed Jasper's hand. "What was that?"

"Just the wind." He patted her hand. "I need to help Lewis with Mr. Barnabas."

"Okay. But hurry back. Don't leave me."

"I won't. I'll be right back with Mr. Barnabas."

Lewis retrieved the carrier, and they went into the bedroom and closed the door. Lewis knelt and looked under the bed.

"Yeah, he's not coming out of there willingly."

"We need to move the bed."

Lewis frowned at the iron bed frame. "This thing must weigh a ton. How about we just move the mattress?"

"Good idea?"

"Every once in a while, I come up with one."

They moved the mattress and the box springs, exposing the frightened cat cowering in the corner.

Lewis held out his hand. "Here, kitty. Get your ass over here, Mr. Barnabas."

Jasper picked up a blanket. "Okay. I'll toss this over him. You grab him."

Lewis looked at Jasper. "Why am I grabbing the cat? You're the chief."

"I don't see how that makes me the one who has to grab the psycho cat. But if you want to change places…"

"No. Just throw the damn blanket." Lewis got into position and Jasper tossed the blanket over the cat. Lewis grabbed the animal as it tried to make a run for it. Jasper held the carrier and Lewis dropped the cat into it.

"Damn cats."

"Don't condemn all cats."

Lewis patted Jasper's back. "All cats except Pepper. How's that?"

"That works."

They took the meowing cat out to Wilda.

"Oh my poor baby."

Lewis frowned and set the carrier next to Wilda. "Do you have food for him?"

"Yes, in the pantry."

Jasper retrieved a bag of cat food and handed it and the cat to Lewis. "Okay, let's get out of here."

He picked up Wilda. "I'm going to put the blanket over you for a minute to protect you from the wind and rain." She nodded, and he covered her up, then went out the door and put her into the backseat of the Bronco. Lewis set the cat, the food, and the purse next to her, before getting in next to Jasper.

Wilda giggled in the backseat. "Oh, my. That was exciting."

Chapter Sixteen

"That's something I never thought I'd say."

Jasper and Lewis got Wilda and Barnabas to the station without seeing any more horses or rolling outhouses. They did get hit by a flying tree, though. It bounced off the side of the Bronco and scared Wilda and Mr. Barnabas. They both let out a shriek.

"It's okay Wilda, just a tree."

When an awning landed on the windshield, Jasper stopped and backed up in a curve, until the wind grabbed a hold of it and carried it off.

Lewis glanced at him. "Keep an eye out for the horses and goats."

"I hope they've found somewhere safe to be by now."

"Is there somewhere safe for them out there?"

"I hope so."

They made it to the station without further incident and Jasper carried Wilda inside, with Lewis and Barnabas right behind them.

Jasper set Wilda in a chair in the reception area, and she ran a hand through her hair. "Oh, my. Thank you."

Jasper laughed. "You're quite welcome."

"Where are we?"

James came from Jasper's office. "How're you doing, Wilda? Are you okay?"

"Oh, Chief. I didn't know you'd be here. She patted her hair, again. "I'm fine. Thanks to these two young men. You raised a fine son, Chief."

James looked at Jasper. "All the credit goes to Kat, I'm afraid. Let me get you downstairs."

"Okay. Don't forget Mr. Barnabas."

Jasper handed the cat carrier to him. James frowned at the cat, but took it, along with Wilda's arm. "Let's go get you comfortable. Have you eaten?"

"Not in a while."

"Kat will fix you right up."

Jasper watched James take Wilda down the stairs, then looked at Lewis. "Thanks."

"Are we done rescuing people? I'd sure like to get on some dry clothes."

"We're done."

Lewis headed downstairs and Jasper tried the phone in his office. It was out. They were officially cut off from the Ice House now and were without power. They were in for the duration.

"Okay, Isabella. Push on through and leave us the hell alone."

He dug through the stuff Poppie packed and took out some dry clothes. He changed into them. He laid his wet stuff over the chairs to dry out. There was nothing more to do upstairs. Isabella would leave when she was damn well ready.

He picked up his guitar and headed downstairs.

The room was set up with beds for everyone. Most of them were pushed against the wall to make room. There were several folding chairs and two picnic tables near the kitchen area. They had several ice chests, two propane cook stoves and several boxes of food. There was also a stack of water bottles, two cases of soft drinks, and a case of beer.

"Thank you, Mellie."

She was pouring herself a cup of coffee and she turned to him. "It's your favorite brand."

"I see that. I also happen to know it's Lance's favorite brand, too."

She shrugged, then smiled as her son came up and put his arm around her waist.

Jasper looked at the boy, who was now in high school. "Weren't you Jensen's age just the other day?"

Mellie shook her head. "Don't remind me. Treasure every day, Jasper. It'll be gone before you know it."

"Scary."

Jasper left them to go to Poppie and the kids. She was reading to them by the light of a gas lantern. He set his guitar in the corner of the cell and sat next to the boys.

Poppie looked at him. "How'd it go?"

"The only casualty was my windshield."

"Tree?"

"Garbage can." He put Tucker in his lap. "We got hit by a tree, too. And saw Bo's horses in the park."

"They came all the way into town?"

"Apparently."

"They must be terrified."

"They were running fast. I hope they find someplace to hunker down."

Jensen put a hand on Jasper's knee. "Dad?"

"Yes, honey."

"What about the goats and chickens?"

"Well, the chickens have a pretty sturdy coop, so I imagine Bo tucked them away inside."

"So, they'll be okay?"

"Probably, yeah."

"What about the goats?"

"Goats are pretty smart. I'm sure they found somewhere to hole up and ride out the storm."

"Maybe Bo will bring them into the cellar with him."

"You never know."

"I would. If we had goats and a cellar."

"I'm sure you would."

Jensen was quiet for a moment. "Can we get some goats?"

"Probably not."

Tucker looked up at Jasper. "Pee."

Jasper shook his head. "Now you decide you want to start using the toilet?"

"Pee."

Jasper stood, bringing Tucker with him. "Okay. Let's go pee."

Poppie watched Jasper take Tucker to the bathroom, then smiled at Jensen.

"If you had a goat. What would you name him?

Jensen took some time to think about it. "Tucker."

"You'd name the goat after your brother?"

Jensen nodded. "That way, I'd never forget his name."

Poppie laughed. "Makes perfect sense."

Sarah came into the cell with Alice in her arms and sat next to Jensen. She smiled at Poppie.

"Well, our wayward men are back safe and sound."

"Hopefully, that will be their last adventure until this is over."

"Knowing your husband, I'd say there's a good chance he'll get the opportunity to play hero at least one more time."

"I know you're probably right, but I hope you're wrong." Jasper returned with Tucker and Poppie looked up at him. "Did he go?"

"Yeah. Just not on the toilet."

"In his diaper?"

"No."

She laughed. "Sorry."

He leaned against the cell door. "Two hours in and I'm already cleaning up pee from the floor."

Poppie smiled at Sarah. "You were right."

Jasper frowned. "Right about what?"

"That you're my hero."

"For cleaning up our son's pee?"

"Yes."

"You guys are weird." He left the cell, and the women laughed.

Jensen looked at them. "What's so funny?"

"I just love your dad so much."

"Because he cleaned up Tucker's pee?"

"Because he's willing to clean up Tucker's pee."

"I don't get it."

Poppie took his hand and kissed it. "You will. Someday, you will."

Jasper, James, Lance, and Lewis made another trip upstairs to check on the wind and the water in the street. James removed the wooden cover over the window on the door, so they could look outside. It was nearly dark, but there was enough light to see the water flowing down the street like a river. It was close to a foot deep but still below the raised wooden sidewalks. It was too dark to see any damage, but the rain was coming down hard now, and the wind was whipping. They'd need to wait until morning. Isabella was still fifteen to eighteen hours from landfall according to the last report they got before the internet shut down.

James covered the window back up, and Lance moved two sandbags in front of the door. Lewis and Jasper rummaged through the stuff the women packed and brought down what they felt was necessary. The rest they put on Jasper's desk.

While they did that, Lance and James picked up everything off the floor and put it on the reception counter and Quinn's desk. Jasper had already boxed up any important paperwork and put it downstairs. They didn't expect the station to flood, but they wanted to be prepared. Tomorrow, they'd check the weather in the early afternoon, then seal the door to the basement and not leave again for the duration of the storm.

As they went back downstairs, Jasper put a hand on Lewis' shoulder. "Did you bring your harmonica?"

He patted his pocket. "Of course."

"I think a little music would be nice to soothe everyone's rattled nerves."

"Sounds good."

Poppie listened from her bed while Jasper sang and played the guitar with Lewis' accompaniment. His singing voice still gave her butterflies, even after six years. She didn't know how she got so lucky, but somehow, she'd convinced him to fall in love with her.

Jensen was sitting next to her and he took her hand. "Dad sings good, huh?"

"Yes, sweetheart. He does."

When they started a new song, Jensen sat up straight. "I know that song. Dad taught it to me."

"Why don't you go sing with him?"

"Really?"

"Sure. You know everyone here. They'd love to hear you sing."

He got to his feet, and walked toward Jasper and Lewis. When Jasper spotted him, he motioned for him to come. Jensen went to him and leaned against his knee. After a moment, Jensen joined in, when it came to the part he'd been taught.

Poppie wiped at her tears. She was extra pregnancy emotional, but it was a beautiful thing. When Jasper looked at her, he winked, and she gave him a nod and watched three of her favorite guys make music and bring down the tension everyone was feeling.

She shook her head and hugged Tucker. "Your dad can't help being everyone's hero."

He looked up at her. "Daddy."

"Yes, sweetheart. Daddy is a hero."

Tucker put his hand to his mouth and blew a loud, wet kiss to Jasper, Jensen, and Uncle Lewis. Jasper laughed when he saw it and stopped singing for a moment to send one back.

Everyone settled down for the night by ten and Jasper laid next to Poppie. Jensen had his own little pile of blankets and Tucker was in the portable crib. Jasper curled his body around Poppie's and snuggled in close.

"Tomorrow and tomorrow night will be the worst."

"When will it be over?"

"By Tuesday, if we're lucky." When she didn't say anything, he added, "It'll still be there."

"Do you promise?"

He kissed her neck behind her ear. "You know I can't promise."

"But you're pretty confident?"

"I'm pretty damn confident, yes."

"Okay. I can work with that."

When she rubbed her stomach and let out a small groan, Jasper put his hand over hers.

"Are you okay?"

"Yeah. Just false labor. Nothing to worry about."

"Are you sure?"

"Yes. One contraction doesn't mean anything."

He rubbed her belly until the contraction ended. "You'll tell me if there's more than one, right?"

"Of course." She sat up. "I need to pee."

"Do you need help?"

She smiled at him. "I think I can handle it."

"Just be sure to make it all the way to the toilet. I draw the line at cleaning up pee from anyone over the age of two."

"I'll do my best."

As he waited for her to return, he studied the cell. He'd actually slept in it a time or two after Ivy and before Poppie. When he got to the point he couldn't bear going home to an empty house, he'd stay at the station and sleep in one of the cells. Those were dark times, and he'd be forever grateful to Poppie for leading him back into the light.

When she came back to the bed, he helped her lie down. He could tell she was uncomfortable. As nice and cozy as Sarah tried to make it, it wasn't their bed at home.

She snuggled into him as best she could and took his hand. "I think I've decided this is the last one."

"Okay."

"Unless you really want to go for four."

He kissed her. "I have everything I could possibly want right here in this jail cell." He laughed. "That's something I never thought I'd say."

"We have our two boys and a beautiful girl. What more could we ask for?"

"Nothing." He raised up and looked at her. "Are you trying to convince me or yourself?"

"As soon as I said it, I was like, wait, is that what I really want?"

"Well, we certainly don't need to decide tonight. Let's get this one out and potty trained, then we'll revisit the fourth baby issue."

"Sounds like a plan."

"Hopefully, Tucker will be potty trained by then, too."

Chapter Seventeen

"Do you have pregnant woman's radar?"

Jasper awoke to the smell of coffee and bacon. He rolled over and stretched. *I love my Mom.* Only she could pull off bacon and eggs while evacuating from a hurricane.

He sat and put a hand on Poppie's stomach. "Did you two sleep okay? I didn't feel you moving around."

"Only because I can't move around." She tried to sit, and he helped her.

"Do you want some more pillows?"

"I want to get up and move."

He helped her to her feet. "Okay. One trip around the room."

"Yippee."

Dr. Hannigan came to the cell door. "How're you doing in here?"

Poppie sighed. "I'm going a bit stir crazy. And my back is killing me."

Jasper took her hand. "I was going to let her take a lap. Is that okay?"

Davis stepped out of their way. "I'm sure it'll be fine. But I want to take your vitals when you get settled back in."

"Okay. This should take us about two minutes."

"Go ahead and take two laps."

"Thank you."

Poppie nodded toward the bathroom. "I need to make a pit stop first."

Jasper waited for her at the door. When she came out, he took her arm. "No running now. Nice and slow."

"I couldn't run if I wanted to."

They walked around the basement, stopping to say good morning to everyone who was up and about. When they got to Kat and Peg in the kitchen area, Jasper took a cup of coffee from Kat.

"Thank you."

Kat took Poppie's hand. "How're you feeling, honey?"

"I've only been on bedrest for four days and I'm going a little bit crazy already."

"Well, I'm sure it doesn't help to be stuck in this basement. I'll bring you some breakfast."

"Okay. Dr. Hannigan is going to give me a once over, but I'll be ready after that. It smells so good. I don't suppose you have any burritos back there."

Kat smiled and nodded toward Jasper. "Thanks to your husband, we do."

"You bought me burritos?"

"I didn't want to go out in the hurricane and break into Steadman's when your craving sets in."

Poppie started to cry, and she wiped her eyes. "Wow. Even burritos make me cry now."

Jasper hugged her. "I didn't want you crying because you didn't have them."

Kat looked at Jasper. "I hope you're in for the duration now."

"Yes, ma'am. As long as the burritos hold out."

They finished their circle before going around again. Then Jasper settled Poppie back into her nest.

"You have the best spot in the place."

"I know. I know." She leaned back against some pillows. "I don't mean to be ungrateful."

Jasper kissed her. "You're not being ungrateful. You're eight months pregnant. You have a right to be a little uncomfortable."

"How about a lot uncomfortable?"

"That, too."

The doctor came to the door, and Jasper kissed Poppie again, before leaving the cell. He returned to the kitchen area and sat at a small picnic table. Kat set a plate of food in front of him, then sat across the table.

"Is everything okay?"

"You mean besides the fact my very pregnant wife and my two young children are holed up in the basement of the sheriff's department while a hurricane is barreling down on us?"

"Yes. Besides that."

"I should've insisted she leave."

"To the mainland? They're going to get hit, too."

"No, to Boston. I should've had Lewis drive her and Sarah and the kids to Priscilla and Steve's."

"Maybe. But you didn't. So now you just need to help them get through the next couple of days."

Even after six years together, insisting Poppie do something made her dig in deeper. Things generally turned out okay, but this was different, and Jasper really wished they'd at least discussed it in more depth.

He needed to take his mind off of it. "So, Mom. Dad said he wrote some poetry when he was in high school."

She smiled. "Yes. Sonnets, actually."

"Right. Was he any good?"

"He was wonderful." She held up a finger, then got up from the table. She returned in a few moments with a folded piece of lined paper. She sat back down. "He wrote this for me."

"You carry it with you?"

"Yes. In my purse." She handed it to him.

"That's sweet. I guess." He unfolded the paper and started reading it, then folded it and dropped it onto the table. "Mother! Good God."

She started laughing. "Honey."

"Jesus. Why'd you let me read that?" He shivered.

"It's beautiful."

"It's X rated."

"Nonsense."

"There are some things sons don't want to know about their parents." He pointed at the paper. "This right here is several of them."

Kat picked up the paper. "I'm sorry. But you asked."

"And I'll never ask anything ever again."

Jasper was still trying to get his father's words out of his head when Davis came to the table.

"When you're done there, can I talk to you for a minute?"

Jasper set down his fork. "You can talk to me now." He stood and they moved to the stairwell. "What's going on?"

"I'm a little concerned that Poppie is so uncomfortable."

"Doesn't that come with the territory?"

"No. She's putting on a brave face, but she's not feeling well."

"Is she going to go into labor?"

"I'm not convinced of that yet. She said she had some false labor last night. I just want to keep a real close eye on her to make sure it's false and not pre-term labor."

"I'll stick by her today."

"Good. But I don't want you to alarm her. Her blood pressure is elevated. Which is understandable considering our circumstances, but I'd like to keep her as calm as possible."

"What do you want me to do?"

"Stay close, but not so close she suspects you're hovering."

"Okay." Jasper looked at the floor for a moment. "If she goes into labor…"

"We'll cross that bridge when we come to it. Although, I wish I'd brought some terbutaline with me. I really didn't think it'd be an issue.

"What's that?"

"It's a drug that slows down pre-term labor. It can hold delivery off for a couple of days."

"Long enough for the hurricane to pass?"

"Yes. Ideally, anyway."

"Do you have that drug in the clinic?"

"Yes." He cocked his head. "It's not worth you going out again to get it."

"Are you sure?"

"Let's give it some time."

"It's only going to get worse out there."

"It's already too bad for you to go out. Let's just keep Poppie calm and distracted. Neither of those things will be accomplished by you going out in the hurricane."

Jasper sighed. "Okay. Calm and distracted without hovering. I'll do my best."

He went back to his meal, but he wasn't hungry anymore. At least now, he had something else to think about. As he was about to get up and return to Poppie, Sarah came and sat next to him.

"What's going on?"

He shook his head. "Do you have pregnant woman's radar?"

"No. I have Jasper's worried radar. What's going on with Poppie?"

"Doc is a little concerned about her. But he's attributing some of her symptoms to the fact we're here and there's a raging hurricane outside."

"What symptoms?"

"She's pretty uncomfortable. More than she should be. Her blood pressure is elevated, and she's been having some contractions."

"Real contractions?"

"Not sure. She says they're Braxton whatever—"

"Hicks."

"Yeah, those. At this point, the doc agrees with her. But he wants me to stick close, but not let her know I'm keeping an eye on her."

"Good luck with that." She put a hand on his arm. "I'll help you. Between the two of us, we can monitor her without her knowing it."

"Okay. We need to keep her distracted. I think part of it is she's bored and frustrated. Uncomfortable. Claustrophobic. God. No wonder she's miserable."

"We'll keep her busy."

Jasper got to his feet. "Okay. I'll take the first shift." He went to Kat. "Can you fix a plate for Poppie?"

"A burrito?"

"Right. Yes. Make it two."

"I could make her a breakfast burrito."

"No. She's set on those frozen ones that taste like crap."

"Okay, dear." She warmed up two burritos and handed it to him. "Send the boys over and I'll feed them."

"Thanks, Mom."

"And, about the sonnet."

He shook his head. "No. Don't. I'd almost gotten it out of my head."

Jasper handed Poppie the plate, then turned to Jensen. "Will you take your brother to Grandma? She's got some breakfast for you."

"Cookies?"

"Maybe after eggs and bacon."

Jensen took Tucker's hand and led him out of the cell.

Poppie watched them go. "How did we get through Jensen's toddlerhood without an older brother to help us out?"

"I don't know. But Gracie will have two big brothers to lend a hand."

"Lucky girl."

Jasper looked at Poppie. "Eat."

"I'm eating. Two? Not sure if I can eat them both."

"Just try. What did the doctor say?"

"He said I seem a little anxious." She rolled her eyes. "Duh. Who isn't?"

"What can I do to make you less anxious?"

"Well, unfortunately, we can't do what I'd like to do. That always works." She smiled at him. "But we can play a game or something."

"Monopoly?"

"No. Not monopoly."

"Twister?"

She started laughing. "Now that'd be entertaining for everyone but me."

"I saw a game of Chutes and Ladders over there."

Poppie shook her head. "Possibly the most boring game in the world."

"Um... Cards?"

"How about Mouse Trap? We can play with the boys when they're done eating."

"Sure. Because that's not a boring game." He got up. "I better go grab it before someone else does."

"Ask Sarah and Lewis and the kids if they want to join us."

Poppie finished her breakfast, then tried to get comfortable. It was impossible. She stuffed a pillow behind her back as she felt another contraction coming. It wasn't a bad one. And once again, she considered it to be of no concern.

When Jasper returned with Lewis, Sarah, and no kids, she looked at him. "What's going on?"

He set down a box of crackers and pulled a deck of cards out of his pocket. "poker."

"Hmm. We're betting crackers?"

"Sure. Why not?"

"And where are our boys?"

"Mom and James, believe it or not, are playing Mouse Trap with all the kids. And Alice is with her grandma."

"Then deal those cards, Mister."

He picked up her empty plate. "Couldn't eat them both, huh?"

"I didn't want them to go to waste. Not after you bought them for me." She smiled at Sarah. "Isn't he the best?"

Sarah batted her eyes. "He's dreamy."

Lewis nudged her. "What about me?"

"You, my love, are beyond dreamy."

Lewis smiled. "Okay. I like that."

Jasper took the cards from the box. "Okay. Enough of the mushy talk. Let's play cards."

Sarah laughed. "You're the last one to talk about mushiness."

"Yeah. Well, I've been schooled by my dad." He shook his head. "Apparently, I'm a novice in the mushiness department."

"What are you talking about?"

Poppie took his hand. "Yes, dear. Is this about the family secret you haven't told me?"

"I don't want to talk about it."

Sarah, Lewis, and Poppie all protested.

"Fine. But don't say I didn't warn you." He looked toward his parents, who were sitting with the boys at a picnic table. "It turns out my dad was quite the romantic in his day."

Chapter Eighteen

"I'm pretty sure your wife is going to have a problem with this."

During their fourth hand of poker, Poppie gasped and rubbed her stomach.

Jasper put his hand over hers. "Honey?"

She nodded and held up a finger. When the contraction passed, she sighed. "Okay, that was a bad one."

Lewis got to his feet. "I'll get the doc."

He left and Jasper put an arm around Poppie. "Are you in labor?"

"I don't know. But that was a serious contraction."

"Not a Hickston...?" Sarah and Poppie both looked at him. "What the hell? I can't remember the damn name."

Sarah moved next to Poppie. "Did it feel like the real thing?"

Poppie nodded. "Yeah. It did."

Jasper got to his feet. "Well, shit."

Poppie looked up at him. "Don't panic yet. It could still not be labor. Or it could stop."

Lewis returned with Davis and Sarah joined Lewis outside the cell.

Davis put a hand on Poppie's stomach. "Was this contraction more intense than what you've been feeling?"

"Definitely."

He looked at his watch. "Let's see if you have another."

Poppie smiled at him. "Would you like us to deal you in while we wait?"

Davis glanced at Jasper. "Scott Haskell told me your husband beat the pants off of him when they played poker. And that was with a partially dislocated shoulder and pneumonia."

Jasper folded his arms across his chest. "Yeah, well, he had a broken leg and never played before, so…"

Davis smiled at Poppie. "Your husband has a way of getting himself into troubling situations more than anyone else on the island."

"Believe me. I know." She reached for Jasper's hand and he sat next to her again. "Somehow, I've managed to keep him healthy for the last few years, though."

"That's true. He hasn't been in the office with an injury for quite some time."

Poppie sighed. "You don't have to wait. One of my three guardians can let you know—" She felt another contraction coming. "No, no, no—" She breathed through it. She looked at Jasper, then at Davis. "I can't be in labor. I just can't."

Davis checked his watch again. "Seven minutes. But it was short. I'm sorry, but I believe you're in early labor."

"There has to be something you can do." She felt the tears coming. "I don't want to have my baby here in this cell, with most of our family and friends thirty feet away."

Jasper kissed her on the temple. "Hon, if Gracie wants to come, there's not much any of us can do about it."

"It's too early. I'm only thirty-two-and-a-half weeks."

Davis patted her hand. "Let's stay calm and see how this progresses. It could very well stop just as soon as it started."

"I know how it's going to progress. I was in labor for six hours with Jensen and four with Tucker. She'll be born before lunch."

Jasper stroked her hair. "Poppie, you need to calm down."

"Please don't tell me to calm down." She laid her head on his shoulder and took a breath. "I'm sorry. I'll try."

Davis stood. "I'm going to leave you alone for a bit. Let's see how it goes."

Jasper nodded. "Thank you, Doctor."

Jasper sat with her through the next contraction, which was ten minutes from the last, then motioned for Sarah to take his place.

Poppie took his hand. "Where are you going?"

"I want to talk to Dr. Hannigan. I'll be right back." He smiled at her. "You can watch me from here. I can't go far."

"Hurry back."

Jasper went to Davis and asked him to go back to the stairwell with him.

"I know what you want to talk about."

"Would the drug delay her labor long enough for the hurricane to pass?"

"Going out there would be much riskier to you, then Poppie delivering the baby early."

"What if I waited for the eye to pass over? That'd give me plenty of time. And it'd be calm. No danger."

"You can't really gauge that without knowing the speed of the hurricane. And if you're out there when the eye passes, you'll be in trouble. As much as Poppie doesn't want to have this baby down here. She doesn't want to deliver without you down here, even more."

"I can base the timing on what we do know. The last report yesterday afternoon had Isabella moving at about ten miles per hour. Depending on the size of the eye, I could have an hour or two. I only need fifteen minutes."

"You have no way of knowing when or if the eye passes over us."

"I can have someone upstairs keeping an eye on the wind and rain. If the sky clears, that's my window."

"I'm pretty sure your wife is going to have a problem with this."

"Will it help?"

"There's no guarantee."

"Give me the odds."

Davis thought for a moment. "Fifty percent."

"Okay. Let me talk to Dad. He knows more about hurricanes than I do." He shook Davis' hand. "Thank you."

"Don't thank me. I'm against this."

Jasper nodded, then left him to talk to James, who was at the picnic table playing chess with Lance.

He sat next to Lance. "Dad. What do you know about the eye of a hurricane?"

"I know you don't want to go out into it. The surrounding winds are the most severe." He moved a chess piece, then looked at Jasper. "Why?"

"Poppie might be in labor."

"Shit."

"I know. Dr. Hannigan has a drug at the clinic that might slow down her contractions. Maybe long enough for the hurricane to pass by."

"What I'm hearing is, you want to go risk your life for something that *might* work for *maybe* long enough. I don't recommend it, son."

"She's only thirty-two weeks with a high-risk pregnancy and she's stuck in a jail cell. It seems to me something that might delay labor is at least worth considering."

"You have no way of knowing when the eye will pass over. Or if it even will. Then you'd be guessing about how long it'll take to pass. Too risky."

"I only need fifteen minutes to get to the clinic and get back."

"I swear son. I'm not sure where this stubbornness came from."

Lance smiled. "Hmm. I wonder."

Jasper glanced at him. "I thought maybe we could take shifts watching the storm from upstairs. If nothing changes up there, then of course I'll stay here."

"And if it does?"

"Fifteen minutes."

Lance put a hand on his shoulder. "I agree with James. It doesn't seem worth the risk. But I'll gladly take a shift watching the weather if you're determined to do this."

Jasper checked his watch. "Isabella probably hasn't even made landfall yet, so no sense going up this soon. I'd say wait until late afternoon."

"Okay."

James sighed. "I'll take a second shift if it's necessary. But I still don't like it. Especially since it'll be dark out there."

"Thank you, Dad."

Jasper got to his feet. "I better get back to Poppie. She's not too happy about being in labor."

He went back to the cell and sat next to Poppie. "How goes the contractions?"

"Every eight to ten minutes. Still only a minute or so long."

"Well, that's good. Right?"

She frowned at him. "How do you figure?"

"They're not getting closer together or lasting longer."

"Yet."

"How about another round of poker?"

Lewis sat in a chair next to Jasper. "Yeah, he hasn't quite won the whole box of crackers."

Poppie took a cracker from Jasper's pile. "What's yours is mine."

He glanced at her. "If you were a better poker player, you wouldn't need to steal my crackers."

"I guess I spent my youth in more fruitful endeavors."

"I don't know. Looks like I have all the crackers, so my misspent youth playing poker is paying off in this situation."

She took another cracker. "Shut up and deal."

Poppie's contractions continued throughout the afternoon, but stayed more than six minutes apart and continued to last sixty seconds or so. The consistency confirmed she was in early labor. But unlike her first two pregnancies, things were progressing slowly.

At four o'clock, Lance went upstairs to keep an eye on the hurricane. There was no way of knowing for sure, but the torrential rains and sideways wind indicated Isabella had made landfall. At least on the island. It had another ten miles to go before arriving on the mainland.

Jasper didn't want to broach the subject of him going to the clinic unless it became a possibility. By late afternoon, he laid down next to Poppie and tried to get her to rest.

He rubbed her back through the contractions and kept track of the time. She couldn't sleep, but she closed her eyes and seemed relaxed between contractions.

He whispered in her ear. "Gracie's going to be fine. She's a big strong girl and when she's ready, she's going to pop right out of there ready to take on the world."

"I can't wait to see her." She was quiet for a moment. "I'd like to wait to see her. But if she's going to come, then I can't wait to hold her. And snuggle with her. And kiss her tiny little toes."

Jasper laughed. "You do have a thing for baby toes."

"They're the cutest thing in this world."

"No. The cutest thing in the world is this tiny little mole behind your ear. And I'm the only person who knows about it." He raised up and looked at her. "Except for maybe Tiny Rum Bottle Guy."

She smiled. "Tiny Rum Bottle Guy never kissed me behind the ears."

"Good to know." He kissed her neck. "There are so many things I want to do to you in a few weeks."

"You mean when I'm sleep deprived and breast feeding?"

"It didn't slow you down the first two times."

She giggled.

When he heard, "Jasper," at the door, he turned to see Lewis. "Sorry to interrupt whatever this is, but I need to talk to you."

Poppie held onto Jasper's arm. "Go away, Lewis."

"Sorry. It's important."

Jasper kissed her, then got to his feet and followed Lewis out of the cell. They went to an unoccupied corner out of Poppie's sight.

"James told me what you're thinking about doing."

"Only if the opportunity presents itself. And as slow as her labor is going, it seems like the drug might work."

"Let me go."

"I'm not going to ask you to risk your life again."

"So you admit it's dangerous and therefore stupid."

"If it'll keep Gracie from being born down here, then it's worth the risk."

"Does Poppie know about this plan?"

"No. I don't want to say anything until the eye actually appears."

When they spotted Lance coming down the stairs, they met him halfway.

"The winds are dying down and the rain has almost stopped."

"It's almost here, then."

"Yeah."

"Let me go take a look."

He went upstairs with Lewis and Lance right behind him. He looked out the window. "Things are definitely slowing down." He looked up at the sky. "Can't see the stars yet."

Davis came up behind them. "How's it look?"

"It's calming down."

"If you're determined to do this, I'll tell you right where to find it. But I still think it's a risk."

"I need to go talk to Poppie."

Chapter Nineteen

"Well, I'm not a...hurricanologist"

"You can't possibly be serious."

"Honey."

"No. Don't honey me. You can't go. I've accepted the fact I'm going to have this baby tonight. I've made my peace with it. I can't make peace with you going into the hurricane again to get something that might not even work."

"It could delay your labor until we get out of here."

"I don't care about that anymore." She put a hand on his cheek. "I care about you. Your children and I need you."

"I'll be gone fifteen minutes. I'll run down to the clinic, get the stuff, and run back."

She looked at Lewis.

He shrugged. "I tried to convince him not to go. You know how stubborn he is."

"If I thought I was in danger, I wouldn't go. You know how cautious I've been since Jensen was born. Doc just said he hadn't seen me in the clinic in years. Unless it was with you or one of the kids."

She looked at Lewis. "Come here." Lewis moved to the bed. "I want you to go with him."

"I told him I'd go by myself."

"Please go with him. I know you'll look out for each other if you're together."

"Of course I'll go."

"Thank you." She took hold of the front of his shirt. "Bring my husband back to me in one piece."

"I will."

"Promise me."

Lewis glanced at Jasper. "I promise."

She put a hand on Jasper's knee. "And you. Bring my brother back here in one piece."

"I promise."

She looked at the both of them. "I hate this. And I swear if you're not back in twenty minutes I'll—" She stopped as she was hit by another contraction. When it ended, she said, "Just go now. Before I change my mind."

Jasper kissed her, and Lewis took her hand for a moment. "We'll be right back."

The men went upstairs and Jasper checked the weather again. He could now see stars above them.

"Okay, here's our window."

They put on slickers, stocking caps and rubber boots, them James handed them each a flashlight.

"Are you sure I can't talk you out of this?"

Jasper put a hand on James' shoulder. "We'll be right back."

"Every time you say that, I believe it a little less. Don't take any chances. If you can't get to the clinic, come back."

"Yes, sir."

James looked at Lewis. "I'm depending on you to keep him from doing anything stupid."

"I'll do my best."

He opened the door, and Lewis and Jasper stepped out into the relatively calm wind. There was no rain, but the air felt heavy, like at any moment it'd burst and release a downpour. It was too dark to see the damage on the street, but they could hear the water rushing. Jasper pointed his light toward the sound.

"That's a lot of water."

Lewis looked at the sky. "So how long do we have before we get nailed by the ass-end of Isabella?"

"At least an hour if I did the math right."

"How are we going to do this? The clinic is on the other side of this river. Otherwise known as, Main Street."

Jasper thought for a moment. "Let's go down a block, and cross after the grocery store. We can stop half-way across on the median if we need to. The three threes should give us something to hold on to."

"Okay. Sounds like a plan."

They walked a block on the raised sidewalk, but had to step off of it between the movie theater and the grocery store buildings. When they were on the other side, they looked across the street.

Lewis shone his light at the flooded street in front of them. "I don't see the trees. The median should be right there."

"Looks like they're gone." He took Lewis' arm. "Okay buddy system. Just like you're walking one of the kids across the street. Don't let go until we get to the other side."

It seemed like a good plan, but halfway across, something big and heavy floated by and knocked Lewis over. Jasper lost his grip on Lewis' arm and barely stayed on his feet.

"Lewis?"

"I'm here. I'm fine. I should've worn a wet suit instead of rain gear."

Jasper found Lewis struggling to his feet with the flashlight a few feet away. "Keep going. We're almost there."

They made it to the sidewalk, and another block to the clinic. They didn't want to remove the plywood from the double-glass doors in front of the building, so they waded around the side and used the rear entrance, which was on a cement platform three steps off the ground. So far that had kept the water from the door. Jasper dug the key out of his pocket and unlocked the door.

Before they went in, Lewis looked at the sky, which was dark. "Um. I can't see the stars anymore."

Jasper looked up and felt rain on his face. "I think we just ran out of time." He opened the door and Lewis followed him inside.

"What do you mean, we ran out of time? You said we'd have at least an hour. It's been fifteen minutes."

"I guess I did the math wrong."

"Jesus, Jasper. Getting the math right was kind of important."

"Well I'm not a...hurricanologist."

"You mean a meteorologist?"

"That too."

"Man. Poppie's going to kill us."

"Come on. Let's just get the stuff and get back." They started down the hall. The building seemed to be intact, with no water inside. "Doc will be glad to hear the clinic is still in one piece."

The clinic pharmacy was half-way down the hall. As Jasper unlocked the door, he heard a sound he couldn't quite identify.

"What the hell is that?"

Lewis shrugged, and looked up, shining his light on the ceiling. They both watched a crack wind its way down the drywall. When it stopped moving and started getting wider, Lewis cursed and pushed Jasper into the pharmacy. But before he could make it inside, the roof collapsed around him.

It took a moment for Jasper to wrap his head around what happened. He put his light on the ceiling above him and found it intact. He looked around with his light, expecting Lewis to be in the room with him.

"Lewis?" No Lewis. He lit up the doorway and found what was left of the hallway ceiling and part of the roof. "Lewis?" Jasper rushed to the door. The debris was blocking half of the entrance. "Lewis? I really can't face going back to Sarah and Poppie without you."

When he heard a, "I'm good. Sort of," Jasper took a breath.

"Are you hurt?"

"Probably. But I can't tell yet. I'm stuck."

"Let me try to get to you."

"Do you still have a roof over you in there?"

"Yeah."

"Stay there. Give me a minute."

"I'm at least going to start clearing the stuff in front of the doorway."

"Okay. Go for it."

Jasper heard Lewis tossing stuff out of his way as he started to clear the doorway. He picked up a large piece of drywall and started to throw it, but stopped.

"Where are you in relation to the door? I don't want to hit you."

"I appreciate that." Jasper saw Lewis' flashlight beam. "I'm right here." He was about five feet away and to the right of the door.

"Okay, I'll clear from this side."

Five minutes later, Jasper could see Lewis. A few minutes after that, he reached for Lewis' hand and pull him out of the rubble. They both lay on the floor for a moment to catch their breaths.

Lewis was laying spread eagle on his back. "I'd really like to go back to the station now."

Jasper slid over to him. "First, let me check you out."

Lewis waved his arms. "I think I'm alright."

Jasper put a hand on Lewis' right leg and Lewis sat up with a yowl. "Shit."

"Sorry." Jasper gingerly felt around Lewis' ankle and up his calf.

"Dammit. Stop. Let's go with it is hurt."

Jasper removed his hands. "Okay. Anywhere else?"

Lewis bent his other leg, which seemed to be fine. "I guess that's it." He looked around the room. "How are we going to get out of here?"

"I'm not sure." Jasper crossed the room to the locked medicine cabinet. "But let me get what we came for first." He unlocked it and used his flashlight to read the labels. When he found the terbutaline, he put the bottle inside a bigger empty one, and put it into his pocket. "Okay. Now. How the hell do we get out of here?"

"Are there any pain pills in there?"

"Does it hurt that bad?"

"I'm thinking along the lines of how much it's going to hurt once we start moving."

Jasper checked the shelves and found some extra-strength Tylenol. He held it up.

Lewis shook his head. "How about some of the stuff you got for your shoulder?"

"I guess that'll be okay as long as you're not drinking."

"Not much of a chance of that happening."

Jasper found something stronger and took two tablets out and handed them to Lewis.

"Do you need something to drink?"

Lewis dug a half-empty bottle of water from a garbage can and swallowed the pills with it.

"That's gross, Lewis."

"It was probably Doc's. He should be relatively germ free."

"So, back to getting out of here."

Since the room they were in had no windows, the only way out was through the demolished hallway. Jasper pointed his light down the way they'd come in. It appeared as though they only need to crawl over about six feet of rubble before it cleared up in front of the door.

He turned back to Lewis. "Okay. We're going out the way we came."

"You should go. I'll be fine here."

Jasper returned to him and held out his hand. "Get your ass off the floor. I'm pretty sure Poppie and Sarah would object to me returning without you."

Lewis took Jasper's hand and let him pull him to his feet. Jasper watched as Lewis tried to put weight on his ankle.

Lewis groaned. "Yeah. That's not happening. So, are you planning on carrying me?"

"If I have to." Jasper looked around the room. In one corner was a stand with canes. "Perfect. Just what you need." He retrieved a plain stainless steel cane.

"Not that one."

"Seriously?"

"Yeah. I want the cool black and silver one."

Jasper put the plain one back and took the black one, then handed it to Lewis. "Are you sure that's the one you want? We have all night for you to decide. Oh, wait. No we don't."

"This will be fine."

Jasper went to the door. "Okay. I think we can crawl along the top of the debris. I'll go first and make sure it won't collapse under us."

"Or you'll be the straw that broke the camel's back and you'll be safe, then it'll collapse under me."

Jasper looked at him. "Do you want to go first?"

"No. Go ahead. I'm kidding."

Jasper entered the space he'd cleared for Lewis then climbed onto the debris. It was raining through the open spaces in the collapsed roof.

When Lewis climbed up behind him, he said. "Is it safe to assume that if the rain has started again, the eye is past us now?"

"That's a pretty safe assumption, yes."

They made their way over the remnants of the ceiling. Jasper tried not to get too far ahead of Lewis, who was moving slower than him with his injured ankle. When he got to within six feet of the door, the debris petered out and Jasper climbed down to the floor. Lewis reached the end and he helped him down.

Jasper approached the exit. "Okay. Let's see what we're up against."

Jasper opened the door, and the wind tore it out of his hands and off the hinges. He and Lewis both watched in silence until it disappeared into the dark.

Lewis nodded. "Oh. Okay. This is what the ass-end of a hurricane looks like."

Jasper started laughing, and it took him a few minutes to get control of himself. "Oh, man. I really do love you, Lewis."

"I'll believe that when we get back to the station. Preferably in one piece."

Jasper chuckled, still not quite in control. "We need a plan."

Lewis hobbled over to him and took his arm. "Are you hysterical? I'll gladly slap the crap out of you if it'll help."

Jasper held up a hand. "I'm good. Just think of the stories you'll have to tell the kids."

"That's assuming I live to tell the story."

"Nah. No worries. We've got this."

Chapter Twenty

"Captain Storm and the Lightning Kid."

Poppie didn't get worried until it'd been thirty minutes. At that point, she tried to get out of bed.

Sarah tried to stop her. "What are you doing?"

"I can't sit here. I need to move."

"Okay. Let me help you." She took Poppie's arm and helped her to her feet.

Davis appeared at the door. "What's going on here?"

"I'm going crazy. I need to—" She groaned and rubbed her stomach. Sarah supported her through the contraction. Then Poppie looked at Davis. "Where's my husband?"

"He should be back any time."

Poppie went to the cell door. "Where's James? James will tell me what's going on."

Davis put a hand on her shoulder. "I'll go get him for you. Please, try to stay calm. You can move around a little, but no more laps. Understand?"

Poppie frowned, then nodded. "Fine. Please ask James to come talk to me."

He left and Poppie looked at Sarah, as her eyes teared up. "I'm sorry."

"For what, honey?"

"For sending your husband out with mine."

"I'm pretty sure neither one of us could've stopped him from going once Jasper made up his mind to go."

Poppie sighed. "Stupid men."

"I know."

"Although, I think yours is a little stupider than mine."

Poppie leaned her head on the metal door frame. "He's so sweet and stubborn. He just can't help himself from trying to save me."

"I know. He's always been like that. If superheroes were real, Jasper would definitely be one."

Poppie smiled. "And Lewis would be his sidekick."

Sarah grinned. "What do you think their superhero names would be?"

Poppie thought for a moment. "Captain Storm. Jasper does have the ability to predict the weather."

"And Lewis could be…Lightning. Captain Storm and the Lightning Kid."

Poppie giggled. "I love it."

Davis returned with James. "What are you ladies giggling about?"

"Our crazy husbands." Poppie put a hand on James' arm as her smile faded. "What's going on out there? Why aren't they back?"

James glanced at Davis. "Well, not sure really." He patted Poppie's hand. "I'm sure they're fine, though."

"What's the weather doing?"

He glanced at Davis again, who gave him a nod. "Looks like the eye has passed on by."

"Which means?"

"It might take them a little longer to get back."

Poppie suddenly felt faint and Sarah, Davis, and James all reached for her as she started to go down.

Davis motioned toward the bed. "Let's get you back to bed."

Poppie laid back on the pillows. "I'm okay, really. I just feel a little lightheaded."

"Let me go get my bag."

Sarah sat next to Poppie and looked up at James. "So, how bad is it out there now?"

When James didn't answer right away, Poppie said, "You don't have to sugarcoat it, James. Just tell us."

"It's bad. I realize my son is stubborn, but he's not stupid. He'll be safe and take it slow. Or they'll hole up somewhere until it's safe."

"Hole up. Like not be here when Gracie comes?"

"I'm sure he'll do everything he can to get back, short of risking his life. You don't want him to do that, right?"

"Of course not."

As Davis returned, Poppie was hit with another contraction and James made his escape.

Sarah looked at the doctor. "They're getting closer together."

He was keeping track of how long the contraction lasted. When it was over, he nodded. "And lasting longer. How's the intensity?"

Poppie sighed. "They're getting stronger."

He looked at Sarah. "I think it's still going to be awhile, but maybe it's time to hang some bedding up to give us a little privacy for when the time comes to deliver."

"I'll get on that."

Davis smiled at Poppie. "I'll come check on you in a little bit."

"Thank you." When he left, she looked at Sarah. "I'm not having this baby until Jasper and Lewis are back."

"They'll be back soon. I'm going to round up some sheets and a helper to make your cozy little nest, a private and cozy little nest."

While Sarah was gone, Kat came to see Poppie. She sat on the bed and took Poppie's hand. "For what it's worth, I tried to talk him out of going. So did James."

"I know. I did too."

"He just loves you so much. He can't help himself from doing anything he can to make things easier on you."

"I know that, too. And once he sets his mind to something. There's no backing down."

"I've got the kids. Sarah's sisters are helping out with them, too. So don't worry about them. You concentrate on yourself and Gracie. And even if he doesn't make it back in time. He'll be here for the next forty years."

"I'll try to relax. But until Jasper and Lewis are back, I don't think I'll be able to."

"I know in my heart he'll get back in time."

"I hope you're right."

"I'm a Goodspeed. We're always right."

"That's what your son keeps telling me.

Jasper and Lewis decided they needed to make it from one sheltered spot to the next, taking it slow and staying safe. Their first move was to cross the flooded space between the clinic and the Hannigan's house.

With Jasper helping Lewis, they hugged the building for a few feet, then crossed the ten feet of space with flowing water up to their knees. When they made it across, they slid along the wall of the house until they got to the porch railing.

Jasper helped Lewis climbed through the rails and they sat with their backs against the wall to rest. Lewis looked at the cane he'd managed to hold on to so far.

"This thing is useless."

"Don't toss it yet. Now that we're on the leeward side of the wind, we might make better progress." He took off his slicker. "This, however, is slowing me down."

Lewis took his off, too. They were both wearing wool sweaters and jackets over thermal underwear. The slickers had done little to keep them dry.

Jasper adjusted his stocking cap. "Okay, the next step is to make it to the other end of the porch."

They stayed low and basically crawled the twenty feet to the far end of the porch, then took another rest. Fighting hurricane-force winds was exhausting.

"At this rate, I'll be lucky to get back before Jensen graduates from high school."

Lewis patted his arm. "We're going to make it back sooner than that. Maybe not soon enough to stop Poppie's contractions. But before Gracie makes her debut."

"Which means this whole little adventure was a stupid waste of time. I should've listened to...well, everyone."

"You're like a dog with a bone when you get an idea in your head. But we all love you for it."

"Next time I get a really stupid idea. Please try harder to talk me out of it."

"How long have we been out?"

Jasper looked at his watch. "I have no idea. My watch stopped."

"Isn't it waterproof?"

"Yeah. Just not hurricane proof, I guess." He looked at the front of the doctor's house. "Doc may have lost his clinic, but his house looks okay."

"Shhh. Don't say that. That's what you said about the clinic right before the roof caved in."

They both shined their lights at the porch roof above them.

"So far. So good." Jasper looked at Lewis. "I'll tell you one thing. There's no one else I'd rather be out here with."

"Thank you. I think."

"You really are my brother. You know that, right?"

"Don't do that. Don't get all sentimental and say things because you think we're not going to make it."

Jasper stretched his legs out in front of him. "That's not what I'm doing. I just wanted you to know."

"In case we don't make it back."

He glanced at Lewis. "I'm sorry you got hurt."

"By all rights, I should be dead after a roof fell in on me. I can deal with a sprained ankle."

"I'll be right back." Jasper crawled to the end of the porch and looked at the distance between the house and the next building. It was about thirty feet and there was a lot of debris in the water. He returned to Lewis.

"Okay. This next one is going to be tricky. Not only is it far across, but we'll be playing dodgeball the whole way."

Lewis leaned back against the wall. "Have you seen the movie *Sharknado*?"

"No. But don't worry. There's a lot of stuff floating by. But I didn't see any sharks."

"That's a relief."

"Of course, they're pretty sneaky, so you never know."

Lewis laughed. "Wouldn't that be something? To get eaten by a shark on Main Street."

"Definitely a story for the grandkids."

"You'd have to tell them. I'd be dead." He nudged Jasper. "I'm ready when you are."

They moved to the end of the porch and Jasper dropped into the water, which seemed to be getting higher. It was mid-thigh now. Since Lewis was a few inches shorter, it's hit him a little higher.

He helped Lewis down. "Watch yourself. It's getting deeper."

Lewis tried to protect his crotch. "Shit, it's cold."

"Just watch out for floating objects and sharks, of course. We won't see it coming in the dark. But if you do see one, you can clobber it with your cool cane."

"I'd like to have the option of having more children if Sarah and I decide to."

"Come on. Just keep moving."

"I've never been more jealous of your height than I am now." He continued to try to protect himself.

Jasper took Lewis' arm, and they slowly crossed the water. Between the current and the wind, it wasn't easy. They'd almost made it without getting hit by any floating objects. But right before they reached the steps going up to the sidewalk in front of the bank, a tree branch floated by and knocked Lewis into the water. Jasper lost his grip and Lewis disappeared.

When Jasper finally got eyes on Lewis, he was in the middle of the street and was getting hit by the full force of the wind. Jasper took off after him and by the time he reached Lewis, they were almost all the way across the street.

"Stay low."

"Is that a disparaging remark about my height?"

Jasper dragged Lewis the rest of the way across and onto the porch in front of the grocery store.

They squeezed it between two large freezers and tried to catch their breath.

When he could talk, Jasper asked, "Are you okay?"

"I'm not sure what hit me, but I'm going to have a hell of a bruise tomorrow."

"Where did it get you?"

"Right leg. On the thigh. A few inches higher…" He shook his head.

"Well, at least it's the same leg. And you can still have children. So look on the bright side."

"Jasper. Take a moment to take stock of where we're at. There is no bright side."

"Sure there is. We made it across the street. We're damn near back."

Lewis took a moment to see where they were. "Grocery store."

"Which is a block away from the station."

"Okay. I'll give you one tiny ray of sunshine."

"Thank you."

Chapter Twenty-One

"Now that the first string is here, I'll go."

Poppie moaned through a contraction, while Sarah and Mellie hung sheets on the two open sides of the cell. Her contractions were getting closer together and lasting almost two minutes now. Having gone through it two times before, she knew it wouldn't be much longer. She also knew once she got to a certain point, it'd go really fast.

As determined as she was to not have the baby until Jasper got back, Poppie was beginning to doubt whether she'd actually make it.

Mellie came and sat beside her. "Is there anything I can do?"

Poppie shook her head. "I just want Jasper." She sat up. "I need to go to the bathroom again."

"Let me help you."

Mellie helped her to the restroom door. "Will you be okay by yourself?"

"Yes, I think so."

"I'll be right here. If you need me, holler."

When Poppie came out of the bathroom, she took Mellie's arm. "My water just broke."

"Okay, back to bed. I'll get Dr. Hannigan." When they got to the cell, Mellie handed Poppie off to Sarah. "Her water broke."

"Come on, honey. Looks like we're going to meet Miss Gracie soon, now."

Poppie started crying again. "I don't want Jasper to miss this. I tried to wait, but..."

"You really don't have any control over the situation."

"Kat said she was sure he'd make it."

"Well, let's go with that. She's his mother. She should know."

Davis came into the cell. "I'd like to examine you now and see how dilated you are."

Poppie nodded.

Now that Jasper and Lewis were getting the full force of the wind, moving was slower and a lot harder. They were able to move about six feet before they had to stop to rest. It took them nearly twenty minutes to go thirty feet to the end of the grocery store. From there, they had to cross the space between the end of the block and the next one. Then past the movie theater to the sheriff's station. They were nearly there.

Jasper looked at Lewis. "One more river crossing. Assuming you don't get hit by another tree, or eaten by a shark, we're about home free."

"I do seem to be a target."

Jasper smiled. "Six feet to the end of the sidewalk. Eight feet across the water, then past the movie theater, which is..."

"No more math. Let's just do it."

Twenty minutes later, they were on the other side of the water, past the movie theater, and a few feet from the door of the sheriff's station. When they reached it, Jasper banged on it and Lance opened it up and pulled them both inside.

"Holy shit. What happened?"

Jasper held up a hand and took a moment to catch his breath. "Poppie?"

"Baby's coming."

Jasper took off his wool cap and sweater as he headed for the stairs. Kat met him at the bottom with a towel. "You haven't missed it, honey."

He ran to the cell and stopped in the doorway. Sarah was holding Poppie's hand through a contraction. He stepped up to the bed when it was over.

Poppie reached for him. "You're here."

"I'm so sorry." He glanced at Davis. "How soon?"

"Anytime now."

Sarah put a hand on Jasper's shoulder. "Now that the first string is here, I'll go. Where's my husband?"

"Upstairs."

"Is he okay?"

"A little banged up. But, yeah. He's fine."

She left and Jasper looked at Poppie again, then took the terbutaline out of his pocket. "I guess we won't be needing this."

Davis took it from him.

Poppie felt the need to push, and Jasper squeezed her hand as Davis talked her through it.

"You're doing good. It's only going to take a couple more."

Poppie tried to breathe before the next contraction.

"I was so worried you wouldn't make it."

"I'm here. Let's get this baby born."

She nodded as the next contraction hit.

Davis nodded. "Good girl. She's on her way. One more big one and you're done."

Gracie arrived with the next push and Davis checked her out, wrapped her up, and handed her to Poppie.

"Is she okay?"

"She's fine. A little small, but she's going to be fine."

Gracie let out a cry that seemed too loud for such a small little thing and Jasper laughed.

"Her lungs sound good." He kissed Poppie, then Gracie. "My God, I almost missed it."

Davis put a hand on his shoulder. "But you didn't." He finished up with Poppie, then left them alone.

Jasper put a hand on Poppie's cheek. "You're so amazing."

"I was so scared something was going to happen to you."

"Eh. We were fine. Piece of cake."

She smiled. "I kind of doubt that. What happened to Lewis? You said he was a little banged up."

"He got in the way of a collapsed roof. Messed up his ankle a little. He also got hit twice by floating debris. But other than that, he's fine."

"Well, as long as nothing serious happened."

Jasper laughed as he looked at Gracie. "Let me hold my daughter."

"You're all wet."

"She just spent eight and a half months in water. I don't think she'll mind." He took Gracie from Poppie's arms and held her up. "Yep, she looks like you. If she could, she'd frown at me and ask me where the hell I've been."

Poppie put her hand on Gracie. "Don't swear in front of the baby."

Jasper handed Gracie back to Poppie. "I believe there are quite a few people out there that want to see this little girl. Let me go get changed, then I'll show her off to everyone."

"Don't go just yet."

Jasper took her hand, and they spent some time making sure Gracie had all her toes and fingers, admired her head of black hair, and marveled over how small she was. When Jasper finally got up to go change, Poppie asked him to send Sarah and Lewis in.

Jasper stepped out of the cell and got a round of cheers from their friends and family. He put a hand on his heart. "I didn't do anything but show up at the last minute. I'm going to go get changed, then I'll introduce you all to Gracie. It was going to be Gracie May. But I think we're going to have to call her Gracie Isabella now."

Jensen ran up to him. "Is my sister here?"

"Yes, honey. She is. I'll take you to see her as soon as I get some dry clothes on."

He spotted Lewis sitting with Sarah. "Sorry I broke your husband, Sarah."

"He'll be fine."

"Poppie wants to see you two."

As Sarah helped Lewis to his feet, Jasper went upstairs to find some more dry clothes. Good thing Poppie was such a thorough packer. He put on dry pants and a flannel shirt over a t-shirt, then went back downstairs.

He picked up Tucker and took Jensen's hand, and brought them to Poppie. Lewis and Sarah were admiring Gracie.

Lewis shook his head. "We did it. We made it back in time. Too bad it was a completely wasted trip. I have a messed up ankle and a bruise the size of Maine for absolutely no reason."

Jasper squeezed his shoulder. "You have to admit, it was kind of fun."

"No. It wasn't."

Sarah helped Lewis to his feet. "Come on. Let's go and give the boys a chance to meet their sister."

Lewis smiled at Jasper. "Ask me in a month or so. By then, I might be able to admit it was semi-fun."

They left, and Jensen sat next to Poppie on the bed. "Can I touch her?"

"Just be very gentle."

Jensen touched Gracie's hand, then her cheek. "I like her." He looked at Tucker. "Look Tuck, we have a baby sister."

Tucker was confused as to what was going on and didn't want Jasper to put him down. Jasper rubbed his back. "It's okay. Pretty soon, you and Gracie will be best friends. And when you get a little older, you'll spend your whole life trying to protect her and keep her safe."

Poppie looked at Jasper. "That's your job."

He smiled. "I figured she's going to be just like you, and it'll take the three of us guys to keep her out of trouble."

"Me? I'm not the one who ventured out into a hurricane. Twice."

"True."

"I imagine everyone is pretty excited to meet our Gracie."

"I'll be right back." He took Tucker out to Kat, then returned to pick up Gracie. "Okay, little one. Let's go meet your family."

Everyone cooed over Gracie, and Jensen made sure everyone knew she was his little sister. When Jasper returned to the cell, Poppie was asleep. He sat in a chair, put his feet up on another, and cradled Gracie. It didn't take long for him to fall asleep as well.

Poppie opened her eyes to find Jasper and Gracie asleep in the chair. She reached over and touched his leg.

"Jasper."

He opened his eyes and smiled at her. "Hey."

"Bring that baby here and lie down next to me."

Jasper handed her Gracie and laid down next to them.

Poppie kissed him. "Thank you."

"For what?"

"For trying. And for getting back in time."

He smiled. "I thought maybe you were thanking me for my contribution in making this little thing."

"Your one minute contribution?"

"Yeah." He looked at Gracie. "Pretty good work, if I do say so myself."

"I have to admit. You do great work in that department."

"Three for three. Not a dog among them."

Poppie nudged him. "Shush."

"So, is Gracie Isabella going to be the last one?"

She lifted her head and looked at him. "Gracie Isabella?"

"We should acknowledge the hurricane's contribution. I don't think Gracie would be here this soon if it wasn't for Isabella."

"Thank goodness this didn't happen during Hurricane Emilio."

"Gracie Emilio. It sort of has a ring to it."

"No. It doesn't."

"Gracie Petunia?"

She laid her head back down on his shoulder. "Stop. Gracie Isabella is all I'll agree to."

"Gracie Isabella it is." He stroked Gracie's cheek. "You didn't answer my question."

Poppie sighed. "I don't know. Ask me in a month or so."

"That means, yes."

"No it doesn't. It means ask me in a month or so."

"Okay. Whatever you say."

"Was it horrible out there?"

"It was wet. And pretty windy."

"Pretty windy?"

"Hella windy. Hella wet. But we couldn't really see how much damage has been done."

"So, the clinic's okay?"

"Um. It was when we got there. But by the time we left, the roof had caved in."

"Oh no."

"Yeah. Damn near took out Lewis."

"But you brought him back safe."

"Yes. I did."

"Thank you."

"You're welcome."

Chapter Twenty-Two

"Wow. I think you missed your calling."

Jasper had his back to Poppie and was enjoying the space between deep sleep and groggy wakefulness when she rubbed his back.

He mumbled, "Behave."

"I can't help it. I love my tall, sexy deputy."

"You just had a baby. We're in a jail cell, with our kids five feet away from us. And everyone we know and love are down here with us. I won't even mention the hurricane outside."

"None of that makes me love you any less."

He turned over and looked at her. "Maybe. But it should make you love me more discreetly."

She laughed. "I know. I'll behave."

He touched her face. "Your hormones are out of whack."

She picked up Gracie and started nursing her. "You're the last one to talk about being discreet, by the way."

"Me? I'm always discreet."

"Eight and a half months ago. Your mother's Christmas party?"

"Hey, I just went into my room to find something to show Lewis. You followed me in there."

"We almost got caught."

"Good thing we didn't." He touched Gracie's cheek. "Or this little one wouldn't be here chowing down like a pro."

"I couldn't help it. Being in there reminded me of the first time I was in your room."

"You wouldn't leave." He put his arm around her. "You were being a snoop."

"Yeah. Then you got out of bed and I saw Deputy Goodspeed in all his glory. And nothing else."

Jasper laughed. "I told you to leave."

Lewis appeared at the cell door, saw that Poppie was nursing, and turned his back.

"Whoa. Sorry."

Poppie laughed. "Lewis, you've seen Sarah nurse all of your children. In fact, she's still nursing Alice."

"I know. But Sarah isn't my sister."

Jasper got out of bed and stretched. "What's up, Lewis?"

James, and Lance, and I are about to go upstairs and see how things look in the daylight.

"I'm coming." He kissed Poppie and Gracie, then looked at Tucker, who was sound asleep. "We can't get that boy to sleep past seven-thirty at home. Here, he's still asleep, and it's almost..."

He looked at his broken watch. "What the hell time is it?"

"Almost nine."

Poppie put a finger to her lips. "Don't jinx it. Let him sleep."

Jasper got a cup of coffee, then the four men, armed with flashlights, went upstairs. The floor was dry, which was a good sign. He half expected it to be flooded, judging by how high the water was in the street last night.

James removed the plywood from the window and looked out.

"Hmm. Can't really see much. The trees across the street are at a forty-five degree angle, though. So the wind's still blowing."

He stepped back and Jasper took a look. "The water hasn't gotten any higher. In fact, it looks like it's receding. That's good, right? The surge is going the other way."

James nodded. "That's good."

"Can we open the door? I'd like to take a look down the street."

James put a hand on Jasper's arm. "Let's give it a few hours. Let the wind die down."

Jasper couldn't see much through the small window, but buildings directly across from the station didn't look like they sustained too much damage.

He stepped back from it. "Okay. You're right. We'll check in a few hours."

Both Lewis and Lance looked through the window before they replaced the board.

Jasper looked at Lewis' cane. "You made the right choice. That one suits you."

"Classy, right?"

They went downstairs and Jasper sat at the picnic table. Kat set a plate of food in front of him. "How's my granddaughter? I didn't hear a peep from her last night."

"Apparently, she's a perfect baby."

"She knows she's loved."

When Poppie approached the table and sat across from Jasper, he smiled. "Should you be up?"

"Yes. I should definitely be up. No more bedrest for me. Gracie is sleeping. The boys are with their cousins. I'm momentarily free to move around."

Kat got to her feet. "There are still some scrambled eggs and sausage."

"Yes, to both." She smiled at Jasper. "How'd it look up there?"

"The floor was dry. Good sign. And the surge is retreating, so we're past the worst of it. Might even be able to go home tonight."

"A day early? That would be wonderful. But let's not rush it. Not with a premature newborn."

"Of course."

Kat sat a plate in front of Poppie and a glass of orange juice.

Jasper looked at her. "I feel sorry for everyone at the Ice House. There's no way they're eating as good as we are."

"Not true. With Thomas, Aaron, and Randy, I'm sure they're doing just fine."

"Yeah. But they aren't you and Aunt Peg."

She kissed the side of his head. "You smell like sea water."

"That would be from rescuing Lewis from the surge. There's probably a little floating debris along with rain water mixed in." When Poppie made a face, he added, "We spent another thirty minutes in the rain, so it probably washed everything disgusting off."

Poppie cocked her head. "Maybe you should take a shower."

"I've spent enough time in cold water the last two days. I'm not going to take a cold shower. I'll shower when we get home. I changed my clothes and washed my hands. It's all good."

"Hmm. I guess so."

Kat laughed. "Well, I guess my work here is done."

"Yeah. Thanks, Mom." He looked at Poppie. "Really, I'm not gross."

She smiled. "I know. Everything around here smells like saltwater."

When they heard Gracie cry, Jasper stopped Poppie from getting up. "Finish eating. I'll get her."

Jasper went into the jail cell and picked up Gracie.

"Hey, now. What's all this?" He put her up to his shoulder and patted her back. When Gracie released a loud burp, he laughed. "Well, I'd cry too if I had that much air trapped inside."

He carried her out to Poppie, who smiled at them.

"She looks happy now."

"One massive burp later."

"You've always been the burp master."

"We all have our talents."

Peg came to the table. "I haven't had a chance to hold that precious thing yet."

Jasper put Gracie in her arms. "Now's your chance before she gets hungry."

Peg took off with Gracie and Jasper sat down and picked up his coffee. "I know it's not even ten o'clock yet, but this has been a good day."

"Any day my husband doesn't go out into a hurricane is a good day."

"I can't argue with that."

After they ate and Poppie fed Gracie, Dr. Hannigan checked them both out. Mother was doing fine, and Gracie, though small—he figured a little over five pounds—was strong and healthy.

He smiled at Jasper, who was standing in the doorway. "You've got yourself a little fighter, there."

"Just like her mother."

"Once we get out of here and I see if my house is still standing, I'll give her a more thorough checkup. If the clinic is compromised too badly and

I can't get to my supplies, I might need to send you to Culver to see a pediatrician. Once the ferry returns, that is. And assuming they faired okay on the mainland."

"Okay. Whatever you suggest."

"You said my house seemed okay, when last you saw it?"

"Yes. The clinic might be a little wet. I hope the rooms on either side of the hallway are salvageable. The pharmacy was intact."

"I'm just glad you boys weren't hurt."

Lewis came up behind Jasper. "You mean hurt worse?"

Davis laughed. "Yes. Hurt worse. How's that cane working out for you?"

"Great. I might carry it even when I don't need it."

Davis smiled. "On that note, I'll take my leave." He left the cell.

Poppie shook her head. "No, Lewis."

"You don't like it?"

"I like the cane. And I like you. But the two of you together. Not so much."

Lewis looked at Jasper. "What do you think?"

"I have to side with my wife on this."

"Dammit. Okay. Sarah said the same thing. Maybe I'll keep it for Halloween."

"There you go. Good idea."

Poppie settle onto the bed with Gracie and Jasper picked up his guitar.

"How about a little music to nurse by?"

"I'd love it. And so will Gracie."

He started playing an old song about love and loss, and Poppie shook her head.

"That one's too sad."

"But the music is beautiful. I'll change the words." He sped up the song and started making up new lyrics. By the end of it, the boys and their cousins had come in to listen, and both Poppie and Jasper were laughing.

"Wow. I think you missed your calling."

"As a songwriter?"

"No. As a comedian."

"I'm here all week."

When Gracie and Tucker both fell asleep at the same time, Poppie wanted to take advantage of the situation and take a nap herself. Jasper tucked them in and took Jensen and the cousins back into the main room.

Jensen looked up at him. "Sing some more, Dad."

Jasper spent another hour singing with the boys. When he was done, he joined Mellie at the picnic table.

She smiled at him. "How about a game of chess, Dad?"

"You know I'm not very good."

She glance toward Lance, who was talking with Lewis and James. "You're better than Lance."

"Alright. But I need to go upstairs soon."

She set up the chess board. "How do you think we did out there?"

He shook his head. "I don't know. Hopefully, the clinic isn't any indication of the destruction."

"I heard about that. I'm worried about how close The Rusty Pelican is to the water."

"Lewis and I were in thigh-high water near the clinic."

"Dammit. Do you think she took on water?"

"She may have." He studied the chessboard for a moment. "No worries. Just open the doors. It'll dry out in no time."

Mellie laughed. "Nothing ever dries out on Gracie Island."

"Thanks for helping with Poppie while I was...out on my misadventure."

"I thought by the time you were thirty-six, your common sense would overrule your emotions."

Jasper shook his head. "Once an idiot. Always an idiot."

She touched his hand. "You're not an idiot. Your only flaw is that you care too much and you have this insatiable need to protect the ones you love."

"Is that a flaw?"

"No. Not at all. I shouldn't have used that word. Poppie and your boys, and little Gracie, are the luckiest people in the world. As are all of us on the island."

"Aww. Shucks."

"I mean it. I never should've left you eighteen years ago."

"If you hadn't, you wouldn't have your son." He glance toward Lance. "Or that stud over there."

She smiled. "He is a stud, isn't he?"

"Everything happens for a reason."

"So if the Pelican is flooded. It happened for a reason?"

"Yeah. It just might take you a while to figure out what it is."

Mellie laughed. "I miss hanging out with you. You're so damn busy these days with the job and all those kids."

"I promise to make more time for you, Mellie."

"Thank you. I'd appreciate it."

He pushed the chest board away. "But we're not playing chess again. I hate this game."

Lewis came to the table with Lance. "We're going to go up again."

Jasper stood up. "Let's go."

The three of them, along with James, headed upstairs and looked through the window. The wind had died down more and it was only lightly raining.

Jasper looked at James. "Now, can we go outside?"

James nodded. "Yes. I think we can take a look."

Lance opened the door and the four men stepped out onto the porch.

James looked up and down the street. "Well, shit."

Chapter Twenty-Three

"Oh, crap."

Jasper felt a little heartsick seeing what the surge left behind. Trees, seaweed, broken lumber, shards of glass, and so much more, littered the street.

The station itself seemed untouched, probably due to its brick construction. But the old marquee in front of the movie theater was on the ground and left a large hole in the porch roof on its way down. The roof over the porch on the building across the street was completely gone.

Jasper put a hand on James' shoulder. "I'm going to go check the Loft."

"I'll come with you."

They headed down the street toward the marina, and Lance and Lewis took off in the other direction to check the grocery store and the clinic.

Jasper was relieved to find the feed store mostly undamaged. He'd be glad to get Blackjack and Sam as soon as he had somewhere to take them. When they got close to the Sailor's Loft, they both breathed a sigh of relief. The building was too tall to see how the roof faired, but the restaurant seemed intact and undamaged. The mast, however, was knocked over and laying across the street.

Jasper put a hand on James' back. "We can fix that." It was blown off the foundation and destroyed the fence around it.

This close to the water, the tide was still going out, and a few inches of water covered the street. As they crossed over, Jasper stopped at the bell lying next to the mast. He picked it up and rang it three times, then carried it the rest of the way to the porch.

James took a breath. "Let's go inside and see if she took on any water."

Jasper nodded, then helped James remove the plywood covering the door. They also uncovered the windows on either side of the door to give them more light. James opened the door and Jasper followed him inside.

The floor in the dining room was dry. Jasper shone his flashlight at the ceiling, and found no sign of water damage. They checked the bar next. Again, the floor was dry, and everything was how they left it.

Jasper circled the bar, and headed for the storeroom. There was a puddle in the middle of the floor from a leak in the ceiling. He put ice buckets under the two visible drips, then checked the stock. Everything seemed to be okay.

He returned to James. "There's some water damage to the ceiling, which means it's coming from the apartment."

"We'll check that after we check your mother's kitchen."

The generator keeping the freezer and the walk in refrigerator running had stopped at some point. Jasper checked the temperature gauge next to the door and found both units still in range. James had left a gas can sitting next to the generator. He filled the tank and started it up.

"We had these replaced not long ago. They seem to hold their temp. Looks like we won't lose any stock."

It was odd to see the kitchen without his mother or Aunt Peg in it. "Everything looks good in here."

"Sure does. Kat will be pleased."

Jasper looked at the stairway door. "I guess we better go see what's going on in the apartment."

James nodded. Jasper opened the door to a puddle of water at the bottom of the stairs, coming from several drips above the stairway. They ran down the steps like mini waterfalls. They climbed to the landing, then down the hall to the apartment door. Beyond the door, their flashlights were unnecessary. The light coming from the six-foot hole in the ceiling was all they needed.

"Oh, crap." Jasper moved under it to take a look.

The branches of a tree, blown there by the strong winds, hung partway through the hole.

"Careful, son. Don't want you to get hit by a tree, now."

Jasper stepped back. The couch under the hole had absorbed a lot of the water.

James looked at the floor and the wet rugs. "We're lucky the whole second floor isn't lying in the restaurant."

The rain had almost stopped. "Must have happened not too long ago. Otherwise it'd be a lot wetter in here. Anything we can do right now?"

"Not until we can get up there and tarp it. Then hope any further rain holds off until we can get the roof repaired."

"By we, I hope you mean me and Lance. I don't think you should go up on the two-story roof, Dad."

"Better me than a new father."

"I bounce better."

"That's probably true."

"We'll send Lance up there. He bounces well, and he only has the one step-son."

"Sounds like a plan."

Jasper looked around the apartment. He'd stayed there when he came back from his training in Augusta. Then, when Poppie moved to town, she'd rented it briefly. He thought about the night of Lewis and Sarah's wedding, when he looked at the bed. After a big fight, he and Poppie had made up that night while the reception was going on downstairs.

James came up to him. "We'll get her put back together. Don't you worry, son."

"I know. I'm just glad the restaurant is intact and ready for business."

"Will you come with me to check the house?"

"Of course. Mom will want to know how it fared."

As they walked the two blocks to the house, they saw a lot of damage, but nothing too catastrophic. Certainly nothing the townsfolk couldn't come back from. The biggest challenge would be removing the ton of debris the surge left behind.

Kat and James' house was closer to the water, and could've sustained some damage. Kat grew up in the house, and so did Jasper. It'd be a devastating loss if badly damaged.

Like the restaurant, they approached the house from across the street.

Jasper touched James' arm. "It looks okay."

The white picket fence surrounding the yard was gone, as were Kat's flowerbeds and most of the trees. But the house was still standing and appeared to be in good shape.

"Looks like grandpa built her to last."

James nodded. "It's a blessing for sure."

They circled the house to check the backyard. The quarter acre of wildflowers Kat planted every spring was flattened, and most of the glass in the greenhouse shattered in the wind. But the frame was still standing. The one big tree in the yard, a giant oak planted by Jasper's grandfather, stood tall only missing a branch or two. But the tire swing was lying on the ground twenty feet from the tree.

James looked around. "Nothing we can't fix."

"Let's go inside."

They removed the plywood from the kitchen door and the window above the sink. They went in and found the house to be perfect inside. They checked every room and found no water damage.

James sat at the kitchen table. "I didn't want to tell Kat her house was gone. That would've been worse than losing the restaurant, I believe."

"You're probably right."

"Seems the only real damage is to the apartment."

"We got lucky."

Jasper got two bottles of water from the pantry. He handed one to James, then sat across the table from him.

"We probably should have our water tested before we use the tap for drinking and cooking."

James nodded. "I'll talk to Davis about that. He's our health department."

As they headed back to town, they started seeing other people checking on the damage. They stopped several times to talk, commiserate, and encourage. They ended up at the Ice House and found Thomas and Maisy out front.

Thomas shook with both of them. "How's it look?"

"We came out alright. The Loft and the house are in good shape. How about you?"

"The café will need some work before we can open. But the house looks good." He looked at Jasper. "How's Poppie?"

"She's not pregnant anymore. Gracie was born last night."

"Congratulations! It all went well, I hope."

"Better than it should've, considering the circumstances."

"Glad to hear it."

Maisy hugged him. "I can't wait to see her."

James took a few steps back. "Kat's waiting to hear the news, so we best get to the station. If you need me or Jasper, you can track us down at the station, the Loft, or home. Probably won't have communication up and running for a while."

"Okay. Take care. We'll give everyone a few days to adjust and take stock, then we'll have a meeting and discuss what needs to be done."

"Sounds good."

Jasper and James headed for the station. Lance and Lewis were there and they all went downstairs.

Kat came up to them. "Tell me."

James put a hand on her cheek. "The Loft is fine, but the apartment took some damage."

"And my house?"

"Your yard's a mess, but the house is untouched."

She hugged James and Jasper. Then she hugged James again before looking up. "Thank you, Dad, for building a strong house."

Jasper left to talk to Lewis. "How'd your end of town look?"

"Not too bad. The clinic seems to be the hardest hit. We didn't leave main street though."

"Do you want to take a drive with me? I want to check on my house."

"Of course."

"Let me go check in with Poppie."

Poppie looked at him when he went into the cell. "The Loft is good?"

"Yes. Except for the mast. But we can put it back up."

"The apartment?"

"Six by six-foot hole in the roof."

"No."

"Yeah. But fixable."

"Still sad."

"I'm going to take a drive and check the rest of town, then drive out to the house if the roads aren't too bad. It might be an adventure getting over and around all the stuff left behind by the high water."

"Just be careful."

"I'd really like to go home tonight."

"Do you think we can?"

"Weatherwise, yes. It's barely raining, and the wind is nearly stopped. It all depends on the house. I'll be back soon and let you know."

She nodded. "Okay."

He kissed her on the forehead and touched Gracie's hand, then went to the boys.

Jensen looked at him. "Are we going home now?"

"Pretty soon. Uncle Lewis and I are going to go check the house right now."

"Okay. I miss my bed."

"Me too." He kissed both boys, before leaving the cell. Lewis was waiting by the stairwell with Sarah, who had Alice in her arms.

"You probably won't be able to get down the road, but if you can get a glimpse of our house..."

Lewis kissed her. "We'll see if we can get close."

"Thank you."

The men left the station and were relieved to find their vehicles relatively untouched. There was a muddy waterline half-way up the doors, and when the water receded, it left them sitting in sandy mud.

Jasper looked at the alleyway. "Now, if we can just drive out of here." The Bronco was in front of the other cars and was the best choice for the condition of the roads. "Let's hope she starts."

They both got in and Jasper put the key in the ignition and turned it over. The Bronco started right up and Jasper let out his breath. "Okay. Thank you, Dad, for this old beast." He drove forward and came out on the next street. It was mostly homes, and they were in varying stages of destruction. But again, nothing too bad. The road was the worst obstacle, and Jasper drove slowly. Several times he had to stop so they could move things to the side of the road. When they got to the edge of town, they headed down the road to Jasper's house. He didn't know what to expect. But he tried to stay positive. Their home had to be alright.

When they drove by his nearest neighbor's house and found it in good shape, he felt better. He went around a bend in the road and caught sight of the house. It was still there. Lewis squeezed his shoulder.

"So far, so good."

Jasper continued on and pulled into the driveway. He could tell the water had gotten close, but didn't look like it got past the foundation. Like his mother's house, there was debris everywhere, but he could live with that.

He stopped the Bronco, and they got out.

"Damn. It's just like we left it."

"It sure seems so."

They walked around to the back. The framed in bedroom suffered some damage. Part of the roof collapsed and some of the two-by-fours were lying on the ground.

"That's about what I expected."

"Nothing we can't fix."

"Let's get the windows uncovered."

They spent thirty minutes removing most of the plywood. A job that took much longer when they put them up in the heavy wind. They cleared the French doors and the back deck, before going inside. Everything was dry, and the ceiling was intact.

"We're coming home tonight." He put his arm around Lewis' shoulders. "All of us. This is your home as long as you need it to be."

"It'd be a lot more comfortable if you'd gotten off your ass and finished the third bedroom."

Chapter Twenty-Four

"So, which one do you want to grab?"

They left the house and headed for Lewis'. But once they got to Harper's Fork, the road was too bad to travel on, even for the Bronco. Jasper stopped and looked at Lewis.

"What do you want to do? I'll hike in with you if you want."

They could tell by the fallen trees and large puddles, the water had only recently receded. Which meant Lewis' house would've flooded with several feet of water, along the other dozen or so other houses on the eastern side of the island.

He shook his head. "I can't right now. Maybe tomorrow."

"Okay. Back to town?"

He nodded. "Back to town."

On their way back, Lewis was quiet and Jasper didn't try to talk to him. When his jovial friend wasn't talking, Jasper knew to leave him alone. They got to town and parked in front of the station. Quinn was there, removing the plywood from the windows.

He stopped when he saw Jasper. "Hey, Chief. How'd you fair?"

"Got lucky. How about you?" Quinn's house wasn't too far from Lewis'.

"Not so much. The house is going to need a lot of work before we can live in it again."

Jasper put a hand on his shoulder. "I'm sorry. I think most of us will be moving out of the basement by tonight. You and Amy are welcome to stay there as long as you need to. I'll try not to arrest anyone in the meantime."

"I might take you up on that. We're staying with the Hannigan's for a few nights, but…"

Jasper smiled. "It's yours whenever you need it. At least I'll have an excuse for getting to the office after you every morning."

"Thanks, Chief."

When Jasper and Lewis went inside, Poppie and Sarah were waiting at the bottom of the stairs for them. Jasper hugged Poppie.

"It's perfect."

She hugged him tight. "Thank God." She glanced at Sarah and Lewis. They were hugging too, but it wasn't with joy and relief. She let go of Jasper and hugged them both.

"Our house is your house. You know that, right?"

Sarah nodded as she wiped at her tears. "It's going to be quite a houseful."

"Which will be lots of fun." She looked at Lewis. "I haven't lived with my brother in sixteen years. So that should be interesting."

"You'll find his manners have improved a lot over the last six years."

"Good. Because he used to be a slob. You should've seen his bedroom when he was in high school."

Lewis frowned. "I think slob is a pretty strong word to use."

Poppie smiled. "Okay. How about excessively messy?"

"Better."

She turned to Jasper. "So, how soon can we leave?"

Jasper put his arm around her. "We can't go jump in the cars and go home. The roads are a mess and for now, the Bronco is the only one of our vehicles that can make the trip. So, Lewis and I should make a couple of runs with all the stuff you ladies packed. And I want to get the dogs out of jail and take them home. So, figure at least an hour or two."

Lewis smiled. "Or knowing the chief here, we'll stop and help a dozen people along the way, so plan on three."

"I'll try to curb my impulse to help. At least until we get everyone home."

Poppie nodded. "Okay. We'll be ready."

"After that though..."

She hugged him. "I know, Chief. I know."

Jensen came up to Jasper and took his hand. "Can I come with you to get Sam and Blackjack? I miss them."

"No, honey, you need to stay here with Mom and Auntie Sarah. You'll see them soon, though."

"Okay. Give them kisses for me."

"I will."

He and Lewis loaded the Bronco with some of the stuff they brought. They figured it'd take two trips for that, and two trips with the family. They'd leave the other vehicles in town until tomorrow or Wednesday, when the roads would be a little better.

On this load, they left just enough room for the dogs. Jasper drove to the feed store and parked out front. There were a few other people picking up their animals as well.

Lewis stayed with the Bronco while Jasper went inside to get the dogs. When he headed downstairs, he was greeted by several barking dogs, all of whom thought it was their turn to go home. He knelt by Blackjack and Sam's crates and looked at Ted.

"How'd they do?"

"They were fine. Pretty quiet, for the most part. Looks like they're happy to see you, though."

The dogs were whining and nosing the door.

"Okay, guys." He let them out, and they squirmed and wiggled and jumped on him. Or at least Blackjack tried to jump on him. "Okay. You ready to go home?" They were definitely ready.

He put a leash on Sam and Blackjack followed them to the Bronco. Jasper gave them a few minutes to do their business, before putting them into the vehicle. Sam in the backseat and Blackjack at Lewis' feet.

They drove to the house and let the dogs out. Sam immediately ran for the beach, smelling everything in his path along the way. Blackjack was happy to stay in the yard, and he too spent time exploring all the new stuff washed ashore.

Jasper and Lewis removed the rest of the plywood and then emptied the Bronco. When they were done, they had a warm beer and called the dogs back to the house.

When Sam wouldn't come, Jasper and Lewis headed down to see what had his attention. They found him pawing at a good sized puddle with two fish stranded in it. Upon closer inspection, they noticed one was a small shark.

Lewis laughed. "I told you there were sharks in the high water."

"So, which one do you want to grab?"

"The one that isn't going to bite me." He studied the situation for a moment, before grabbing the non-shark by the tail and carrying it to the water.

Jasper frowned at the baby shark. "Okay. I'm doing this to help you. I could just leave you here, you know." He took a breath, then picked it up by the tail. The shark wasn't happy and didn't seem to appreciate Jasper's help. It tried its best to take a chunk out of Jasper's arm as he ran for the surf, cursing the whole way.

Lewis laughed as Jasper waded a few feet into the water and let the shark go.

"Good job, chief.

Jasper checked his arm for damage. "The bastard damn near got me." He whistled for Sam, who had followed the fish into the water. "Come on, boy. Now you're wet."

As they headed for the house, Jasper glanced at Lewis. "If you want to stay here, I can bring Sarah and your kids next. Then I think one more trip will do it. I'll load up the back, leaving room for the boys and Gracie. We can get the rest tomorrow."

"Okay, sounds like a plan."

"I'm going to check on Duke. His dad's place is right up the road, and then Bert. So give me thirty."

"Okay. I'll be here. I'll clear the driveway off."

"Cool, thanks. Keep Sam outside until he dries off a little."

He finished his beer, tossed the empty can to Lewis, then with a wave, he got into the Bronco and pulled away.

Duke's father's place was a few miles from Jasper's down a side road. Jasper made the turn, but could only go half-way before he was stopped by a tree across the road. He parked the Bronco and walked the last quarter mile.

The house looked okay except for the tree leaning against the porch. He stopped in front of the house and called out.

"Duke? It's Jasper. Just checking up on you."

When he got no response, he went onto the porch and knocked on the door. "Duke? You in there?"

He was about to try the door when he heard a noise coming from the side of the house. He stepped off the porch and followed the sound. The doors to the root cellar were thrown open and Duke was climbing out. He gave Jasper a crooked smile.

"Hey, Chief. Is it all over?" He was obviously intoxicated, and Jasper couldn't help but smile.

"It's over, Duke. You can come out."

Duke stumbled the rest of the way out, looked at the beer can in his hand, then put it behind his back. "What are you doing here?"

"Making sure you're alright."

Duke gave him a thumbs up. "Fine. I thought it was going to last until Monday."

"It is Monday. Actually cleared out before we thought it would."

"It's Monday?"

"Yep."

"What happened to Sunday?" He walked around the house and spotted the tree laying against his porch. "Well, shit."

"I just wanted to make sure you were okay."

"I'm good. My Dad's house, not so much."

"The road is blocked by a tree a quarter mile down. You'll need to move it before you can get your truck out."

"Okay. I'll get the chainsaw."

"Save it until tomorrow, Duke. Don't do it today."

He held up his beer. "Right. Good idea." Jasper turned to go, but stopped when Duke asked, "How's the marina?"

"I haven't looked at it yet."

"Okay. See you, Chief."

Jasper walked back to the Bronco, then drove into town. He met a few people on the road and stopped to talk to them before going to Burt's house. Like on Friday, Burt didn't answer the door. Jasper went in, and stomped on the cellar door.

"Burt. It's Jasper. Are you okay?"

The door lifted and Burt peered out. "Chief?"

"Yeah. It's all clear. You can come out now."

"It's over?"

Jasper nodded. "It's safe to come out. Your house looks fine. You might need a few shingles, and you lost a tree, but otherwise looking good."

"Thank you, Chief."

"You're welcome. I'll get someone over here in the next few days to help you with the tree and to check your roof."

"Okay."

"You take care, Burt."

"Okay."

Jasper left Burt's house and returned to the Bronco. He used the streets this time to get to the station, so it took a little longer than it had on Saturday. Again, he stopped to talk to people along the way. Everyone seemed to be in pretty good spirits, considering what they'd gone through. He figured once the enormity of the cleanup hit them, the mood might change a little. But Gracie Islanders were tough. They'd be fine, and they'd do what they needed to do.

When Jasper got to the station, he found James and Quinn at the radio behind Maisy's counter.

"Any luck?"

James glanced at him. "No. You'll need to have someone check the tower tomorrow. It'll probably be the first thing we can get going, though."

The radio tower was on top of the station. "I'll send Lance up tomorrow if he's free."

"The phone lines will take a little longer. Gonna need someone from the mainland to come out and fix that problem."

"I'm sure they'll have their hands full for a while. We won't be their first priority."

Quinn turned to Jasper. "My uncle is retired from the phone company. I can ask him to come take a look."

"That'd be great. Thanks."

"Of course, I don't know how I'll get a hold of him. I'll have to wait for the ferry to start and go to Culver to call him."

"No matter how long it takes, it'll be faster than waiting on the phone company. I'm going to load the Bronco, then get Sarah and the kids. They'll be staying with Poppie and me for a while."

"Did he flood?"

"Yeah. It's pretty bad. He's closer to the shore than you are."

After loading the Bronco, Jasper headed down the stairs and found Poppie, Sarah, and the kids to be the last of the evacuees.

"Where is everybody?"

"All gone. Some might be back if they can't stay in their homes."

"All in all, it's not too bad out there." He picked up Tucker and gave him a kiss. "We managed to get it down to three trips. So Lewis is at the house and I'll bring Sarah and the kids first. Then I'll be back for the rest of you."

Jensen tugged on his pant leg. "I want to go now."

"Just a little while longer, I promise. You need to stay here with Mom, and Tuck, and Gracie. There aren't enough seatbelts. Too many kids!"

Jensen sighed. "Okay."

Micha came over to them. "Uncle Jasper. He can go, and I'll stay here with Auntie Poppie."

Jasper patted his head. "That's nice of you." He glanced at Sarah. "As long as it's okay with your mom."

"Sure. Thank you, honey."

Jasper set Tucker down. "Okay. We all good?"

Poppie smiled. "Just hurry back."

Chapter Twenty-Five

"This is the real world."

Jasper dropped Sarah and the kids off with Lewis and unloaded the Bronco, then headed for town. Poppie and the remaining kids were waiting upstairs for him when he got to the station. He found Maisy and Thomas there, talking with James and Poppie.

Maisy had Gracie in her arms. "Jasper, this is the most beautiful baby I've ever seen."

Thomas looked at her. "You probably shouldn't mention that to Aaron and Randy."

"My boys were beautiful too, but this little thing is precious."

Jasper smiled at Gracie. "You've got that right, Maisy."

Thomas shook his head. "All right, honey, let's go and let these folks get home." He just seemed to notice Micha. "I don't think this little one here is a Goodspeed."

Jasper laughed. "They're all interchangeable. Goodspeed, Jensen. One giant noisy family." He picked up Tucker. "Let's go home."

Poppie didn't fully believe the house was fine until she saw it for herself. She took a breath and reached for Jasper.

"It's really okay."

"Did you think I was lying about it?"

"No. I just had to see it myself."

As they pulled up to the house, Lewis and Jensen were in the drive moving debris. Jasper stepped out of the car.

"Good job, guys. It's already looking better."

Jensen ran to him. "Uncle Lewis said we can have a giant bonfire with all the junk."

"Sounds like a plan. As soon as it dries out a little. Right now, we'd just have a giant puff of smoke."

Jensen giggled. "That'd be cool."

"Yeah, not really." He got the two boys out of the Bronco and helped Poppie and Gracie up the porch steps.

She frowned at him. "I'm not helpless."

"Will you just let me take care of you for a day or two?"

"You always take care of me."

"You'd think by now you'd get used to it."

She kissed him, then stopped in front of the door. He smiled and opened it for her. Gracie was asleep, so she took her into the bedroom and put her into the bassinet beside their bed.

Jasper came up behind her. "Sorry I didn't get her room done before she got here."

Poppie tucked the blankets around Gracie. "It's okay. She'd be in here for a while, anyway."

"Yeah. But now I basically need to start over."

She turned to him and put her arms around his neck. "You've got a lot to deal with for the next several months. Gracie's room can wait until spring."

"Speaking of which, Lewis wants to take a look at the marina."

She patted him on the chest. "Go. We're home. You go do what you need to do. I've already come to terms with the fact you won't be around too much for the next couple of weeks. The town needs you."

Jasper kissed her. "Have I told you lately how much I love you?"

She thought for a moment. "I don't believe you have."

"Hmm." He backed up and started to leave. "I'll have to do that soon."

"Jasper Tucker Goodspeed. Get your butt back here and tell me how much you love me."

He went back to her. "I love you more every day. Every morning, I'm like, okay. This is it. It can't get any better than this. But it always does."

"You should write greeting cards."

"I'd consider it if anyone sent cards anymore."

"Around here, we can't even get an e-card."

"What's an e-card?"

"It's what they send in the real world."

"Not interested, then." He kissed her forehead. "And as far as I'm concerned. This is the real world."

Jasper and Lewis said, "shit," at the same time when they saw the marina. Jasper parked in the lot and they walked toward the pier. It was a tragic sight. A few boats were partially sunk and more were listing heavily to the side. There were five smaller craft that had been blown onto land, or rode the surge in. It was hard to tell. But they were now high and dry. The main pier seemed relatively unharmed, but it was covered by debris, like everything else. The other smaller piers were in varying degrees of disrepair.

Jasper put a hand on Lewis' shoulder. "Looks like you're going to be busy for a while."

"I don't even know where to start. This goes way beyond scraping hulls and varnishing woodwork."

"Start with whoever gets their insurance money first."

"Sounds like sound business advice."

Several of the boat owners were milling around. The whole atmosphere was one of shock over the enormity of the work it was going to take to get back to normal.

When Lewis started searching for something, Jasper asked, "What's up?"

"The Buttercup."

"Buttercup?"

"I was talking to Russ a couple of weeks ago about buying it." He spotted it on land near the marina office. "Crap."

They walked over to it, then circled it.

Jasper knelt and looked at the hull. "It seems to be in one piece."

"Yeah."

Jasper smiled. "Might be able to get it at a good price now."

"Wow. You want me to take advantage of Russ' misfortune?"

"No. Of course not. He just might not want to deal with getting it back to the water."

"I'm not sure I want to deal with getting it back on the water."

"Since when have you been thinking about getting a boat? And why haven't you said anything?"

"I know how you feel about boats and the ocean. I figured you try to talk me out of it."

"Just come home safe whenever you're out there. I don't want to ring the bell four times when I go to the Loft."

"Don't worry. I'd never do anything stupid like chasing after a murdering kidnapper into a hurricane."

"Yeah. That'd be really stupid."

As they passed The Sailor's Loft, they noticed the door was open.

"Mom must be inside."

They went up the steps and Jasper rang the bell, which was now hanging from a nail next to the door. The restaurant was almost filled to capacity. Peg came from the kitchen with an armload of plates. After dropping them off, she hurried over to Jasper and Lewis.

"Thank goodness. We can use your help."

Jasper looked around. "What's going on here?"

"A lot of folks either don't have a kitchen to go to, or their appliances aren't working. We opened the place up for whoever needs a meal."

Jasper hugged her. "That's amazing."

"Those that can pay, do. Others are trading salvaged food supplies. And for those that can't do either, there's a jar on the counter for donations." She smiled at him. "You know what we do here on the island."

He nodded. "We take care of our own."

"Grab an apron."

Jasper and Lewis spent the next several hours serving food. For those that could pay for it, they served alcohol. Food was a necessity. Alcohol wasn't. At nine o'clock, Kat closed down the kitchen and left a note on the door announcing she'd be open at eight in the morning.

For the last hour or so, Jasper had been behind the bar. Kat came in to see him.

"You don't need to stay open, honey. Leave when you want. I'm sure Poppie's wondering where you are."

"Lewis ran home around seven to let the ladies know what we're doing. I'll stay open until ten. There's a lot of goodwill and commiserating going on. Might as well give them a place to do it."

"Thank you, sweetheart. Lewis is helping with the dishes. I'll send him to you when he's done."

"Go home and get some sleep. I'll see you in the morning."

"Good night, honey."

"Love you."

"I love you more."

Jasper served the Murphy brothers their third beer. Their boat had suffered some damage, but they'd be back on the water sooner than a lot of the other fishermen would.

"I'm cutting you guys off after this one. I really don't have the strength or inclination to deal with a Murphy brother dust up tonight."

"You got it, Chief. We're headed home after this one."

Duke was at the end of the bar and Jasper walked over to him. "I didn't see you come in."

"I've been at the marina all evening. It seems like an impossible job to clean it all up."

"What can I get you?"

"Coffee. I drank enough over the last two days." Jasper poured him a coffee and set it in front of him.

"Is your office okay?"

Duke shook his head. "Got a foot of so of water inside. Fortunately, I got everything off the ground before I left it. I lost my damn boat, though."

"Oh, man. I'm sorry."

"Yeah. It's twenty feet from the water with a hole in the side."

"Fixable?"

"Don't know."

Jasper patted his arm. "We'll get through this."

He left to pour a few more beers, then spotted Lewis approaching the bar.

"If it isn't the best damn waiter on Gracie Island."

Lewis held up a finger. "And dishwasher."

"Can I get you a drink?"

"Nah." He looked around the bar at the twenty or so patrons. "How much longer are you going to be here?"

"I'm working on getting them out of here."

"I think I'll go try to start the SUV. If I'm not back, it means I made it."

"Okay. Tell Poppie I'll be home soon."

Lewis nodded. "Keep an eye out for me on the side of the road."

"Will do."

After Lewis left, Jasper noticed some Pelican regulars come in.

"Evening fellas. What can I get you?"

The three men ordered beers, then told him the Pelican had sustained some damage and wouldn't be open for a few days.

"Well, you're welcome here, as long as you go back to Mellie when she's open. I don't want her accusing me of stealing her customers."

One of the men laughed. "Don't worry, Chief. This place is way too calm for us."

The bar finally emptied out by ten and Jasper closed up. Before heading home, though, he drove by The Rusty Pelican. The lights were on, so he parked and went inside. He found Mellie and Lance cleaning the floor, which had a thick layer of wet sand covering it.

They both stopped and looked at him when he came through the door.

He smiled. "You could always start selling mai tais, pina coladas, and mojitos with little umbrellas in them. Then you could leave the sand."

Mellie leaned on her shovel. "I'll take that under advisement. If you're here to harass me, go home to your wife. If you're here to help, then pick up a shovel."

"I'd love to help, and tomorrow, I will. But I haven't seen my wife and kids for about six hours, so I really need to go home."

She smiled. "Good job, Chief. You didn't let your insatiable need to help, stop you from doing what you know is the right thing to do."

Lance nodded. "Yeah. Don't worry. There will still be plenty of sand here tomorrow. Assuming I can drag Mellie's ass home soon."

"I'll be back." He pointed at Mellie. "Go home."

When Jasper got home, the kids were all asleep and Lewis and Sarah were on the couch talking.

Lewis looked at him. "He's back before midnight.

"I didn't want to turn into a pumpkin. Or lose my shoe. However that goes. I'm too tired to be clever right now."

Sarah smiled. "Go to bed. This is just the first of many long days ahead."

Jasper nodded. "Sleep well."

He found Poppie on the bed with a book, and Gracie asleep in her bassinet. Jasper went to look at her for a moment, then laid on the bed.

Poppie kissed him. "You look exhausted."

"I'm so glad to be home."

"And like you promised, it's all in one piece."

"We got very lucky. Our house, Mom's house, the Loft."

"I love that Kat and Peg opened the restaurant tonight."

"It really helped everyone feel like things will be fine."

"With you and your parents, Quinn, Lance, even my dear brother Lewis. It's all going to be okay, isn't it?"

"Yes. It is." He yawned and closed his eyes.

"Sweetheart. Get undressed before you fall asleep."

He grumbled. "I'm too tired."

"Jasper. Do what you're told."

He smiled. "Fine." He got to his feet and undressed.

"Do you have to pee?"

"No, ma'am."

"Okay. Come to bed."

He laid down and Poppie snuggled up next to him.

"Our first night home."

He yawned again. "We were only gone for two nights."

"I know, but it seems so much longer." Gracie fussed, and she started to get up.

Jasper stopped her and mumbled, "I'll get her."

"I appreciate the offer, my very tired husband, but I have what she wants." She got out of bed and went to the bassinet.

"Yeah. And I want them back when she's through with them."

Poppie changed Gracie, then picked her up and bounced her for a moment. When she felt Jasper looking at her, she smiled.

"What?"

"I love you in newborn baby mode."

"It is a special time. And it goes by so fast."

"Come feed her in bed."

"I thought we agreed not to do that with the boys."

"We did. But his is Gracie. And she might be our last. Bring her to bed."

Chapter Twenty-Six

"And all is right with the world, again."

Jasper was sitting at his desk, going over the mounds of paperwork the destruction from the hurricane had caused. He was trying to match the list of requests to the lists of volunteers and donations.

He looked up and saw Micha and Jensen watching him. He cleared his throat, and they did the same. "Okay, you little monkeys. Do you want to get out of here for a little bit?"

Jensen slid off his chair. "Can we go see mommy?"

"At home?"

"No. She's with Grandma."

This was news to Jasper. He'd left her at home with Sarah and the younger kids.

"How do you know that?"

"When we got lunch with Maisy, we saw her."

Jasper stood. "Okay, men. Let's go investigate."

The boys followed Jasper to the reception area and got a smile from Maisy. "Where are you boys headed to?"

"Is my wife at the Loft?"

Maisy smiled slyly. "She might be. She told me not to tell you unless you specifically asked."

Jasper shook his head. "If you need me. You know where to find me."

He and the boys walked to the restaurant. The weather since the hurricane had been sunny and warm. It'd only been a week, but things were getting back to normal.

When they got to the Loft, Lance and James, along with the help of Earl and his lift bucket, were putting up the mast.

Jasper stopped the boys a safe distance away until James waved them through.

"Come on ahead."

"Do you need some help with that?"

"No. We've got it."

They continued to the porch and the boys argued over who got to ring the bell. Jasper let them each ring it once, then he added the third one. They went inside, and Kat came to greet them. She kissed them all.

"Hello, my three handsome boys. Are you here to eat?"

"I heard a rumor my wife was here."

Kat smiled. "She's behind the bar."

Jasper shook his head. "That woman. Do you think you could find something for these two to eat while I go talk to Poppie?"

Kat took the boys' hands. "Of course. How about some ice cream?"

Jasper went to the bar and found Poppie pouring two drafts. When she turned around, she had Gracie in a carrier on her chest. Jasper couldn't help but laugh.

Poppie spotted him and walked over. "Hey, Chief."

"I got a report of an underage person in the bar."

Poppie patted Gracies' back. "Hmm. I haven't seen anyone fitting that description."

"What are you doing here?"

"There was no one to work today. Kat and Peg have been covering the bar, but they're busy in the restaurant."

"Did they call you?"

"No, I called to see how they were doing. They're still feeding about a third of the town."

Jasper went behind the bar and put his arms around her and Gracie. "I love you." He kissed Gracie on the head.

"You're not mad?"

"How could I be mad? You're here, with our daughter, behind the bar serving drinks."

"Only on Gracie Island." The baby started to fuss. "Can you stay a few minutes? I think this girl is hungry."

"I've got it. Go."

After Poppie fed Gracie, she and Jasper worked the bar together for another hour. Then Beryl came in to take over until Mark came in.

"You two go. Take a walk or something."

"Thanks, Beryl."

They left to find the boys, who were helping Grandma and Peg in the kitchen.

Peg smiled at them. "Please don't take these helpers away."

"Are they working off their ice cream?"

"Yes. They really are. And more. You two go take a few minutes. Take a walk or something."

Jasper looked at Poppie. "Everyone wants us to take a walk."

"I guess we better take a walk, then."

They went through the front door and the mast was standing and secured. James handed Jasper the bell. "Will you put this where it belongs, son?"

"I'd be honored." He took the bell and hung it from the mast, then straightened the sign, which had been re-touched by Beryl.

He put a hand on Gracie and read it to her.

"Twilight and evening bell

And after that, the dark!

And may there be no sadness of farewell.

When I embark."

He put an arm around Poppie's waist. "And all is right with the world, again."

They continued on their walk and headed for The Rusty Pelican. Mellie was there with a few helpers, getting ready to open.

"Hey Chief. Mrs. Chief. Little tiny baby deputy."

Jasper looked around the bar. "Looking good, Mel."

"I'll be opening in an hour."

He nodded. "It should be a crazy night. I'm sure Mark will be glad to be rid of your ruffian customers."

"Don't disparage my customers. They spend a lot of money here. And I just spent a ton putting this place back together."

"Have a good night and call me if you need me."

They left the Pelican and headed for the marina. Considering how bad it was a few days ago, it looked good. The boats that were high and dry had been hauled back to the water if they were sound, or put into dry dock if they needed to be repaired. The damaged boats along the pier were being pumped out or had been hauled away if they were beyond repair.

Duke's office was airing out and he was back at his post as harbor master.

Lewis spotted Jasper and Poppie and came to say hi.

"How'd you manage to get away without any kids?" He glanced at Gracie. "Almost no kids."

"Your wife has a few, And Aunt Peg put the other two to work."

"Good. It's about time they earned their keep."

"It's looking good here. Quite a turnaround in just a few days."

"Everyone wants to get back to work. And they need their boats to do that."

Jasper put a hand on his shoulder. "Good thing we have a master boat builder in residence."

"I don't know about master."

Poppie smiled. "You will be when you're through with all this."

"Alright. Enough visiting. I've got to get back to work. Go enjoy yourselves. This no kid thing isn't going to last long."

"We'll see you at home." They started walking, then Jasper stopped and turned back. "Speaking of earning your keep. Bring home something from the deli for dinner. They got their kitchen running today."

"Yes, sir, Chief. I'm on it."

Jasper and Poppie left the marina and as they got near the sheriff's station, they spotted Quinn on the roof.

Jasper waved at him. "How's it going?"

"We're about thirty minutes away from having radio service again."

"Great news. Don't fall off of there. I don't want to have to train a new deputy."

"I'll try."

Poppie looked at Jasper. "Where to now?"

"One more stop."

"Where?"

"Come on."

They continued on to the park. A group of volunteers were cleaning up the last bit of debris from the grass. There were still a few downed trees to deal with. But like the rest of the town, it was getting back to normal.

Skeeter McDonald came over to them.

"What do you think?"

"It looks great. How's the ballfield?"

"Should be able to play by next weekend."

"I'm ready."

Jasper and Poppie crossed the grass to the gazebo. The top section was missing, but the platform and the bottom half was intact. They climbed the steps and sat on the bench.

Poppie laid her head on his shoulder. "Chief Goodspeed, your town is coming together."

"Yes it is."

"I don't suppose you have a Cobb salad and some brownies on you."

He kissed her hair. "I wish I did."

She sighed. "I think I've come to a decision."

"About what?"

"Gracie deserves to have a baby sister."

"Hmm. That was record timing."

She glance at him. "What do you mean?"

"Gracie is negative four weeks, and you already want to have another baby."

"Not right away."

"A couple years?"

She laid her head back down on his shoulder. "Yes. When she's potty trained."

"Because that plan worked out so well with Tucker."

"What do you think?"

"It could end up being a baby brother."

She kissed his neck. "That's okay. Gracie and I against four men. We can handle it."

"I'm sure you can."

"So...?

"Sounds like a plan."

"You might want to have the addition built by then."

"I'll get right on that."

More Books By Leigh Fenty

The Three Oaks Ranch Series

Memories Of You

The Good Son

The Wayward Son

Little Sis

The Carmichael Series

Deacon

Tobias

Abligale

Tanner

The Christmas Wedding

Faith's Journal

The Gracie Island Series

The Deputy
The Best Woman
The Chief
The Family Man
The Visitor

About the Author

Leigh spends her days with cute, sexy guys. Unfortunately, they're on paper. But still, not a bad way to spend your day. She also writes about strong, independent women, who can hold their own against these irresistible guys. She's not a pure romance writer, because she breaks the rules a bit. But that's the fun part. Leigh's stories have adventure, family relationships, and the struggles life throws at you sometimes. But boy always meets girl. They tussle a bit while they figure out what they really want. Then find their happily ever after. Even if it's not what they thought it was going to be.

Made in United States
Orlando, FL
02 June 2024